"There's Seducing
And Then There's *Seducing*,"

Sam explained.

"Really?" Laura's eyes widened in a deliberate show of astonishment as she placed her elbows on the table and leaned forward. "Tell me more. The mind boggles."

"The mind may boggle, but it's the body...the body that gets stroked and touched, kissed and licked."

"Licked?" she croaked, aroused by the ravishing roughness of his voice.

"Mmm, like this." Sam brought her hand to his mouth. When his tongue flicked the delicate web between her thumb and her index finger, she was amazed at the pleasure that radiated through her.

"And here." Raising her wrist to his mouth, he used his tongue the way a magician uses his wand—to create magic. Black magic. The kind used to cast spells and charm maidens into surrendering.

She was hooked.

Dear Reader:

Welcome to Silhouette Desire—sensual, compelling, believable love stories written by and for today's woman. When you open the pages of a Silhouette Desire, you open yourself up to a whole new world—a world of promising passion and endless love.

Each and every Silhouette Desire is a wonderful love story that is both sensuous *and* emotional. You're with the hero and heroine each and every step of the way—from their first meeting, to their first kiss . . . to their happy ending. You'll experience all the deep joys—and occasional tribulations—of falling in love.

In future months, look for Silhouette Desire novels from some of your favorite authors, such as Annette Broadrick, Dixie Browning, Kathleen Korbel and Lass Small, just to name a few.

So go wild with Desire. You'll be glad you did!

Lucia Macro
Senior Editor

CATHIE LINZ
SMILES

SILHOUETTE *Desire*

Published by Silhouette Books New York

America's Publisher of Contemporary Romance

SILHOUETTE BOOKS
300 East 42nd St., New York, N.Y. 10017

ISBN: 0-373-05575-7

First Silhouette Books printing June 1990

Printed in the U.S.A.

CATHIE LINZ

is currently celebrating her tenth anniversary as a full-time author of contemporary romantic fiction, which is quite a change of pace from her previous career in a university law library. An avid world traveler, Cathie often uses humorous mishaps from her own trips as inspiration for her stories. However, the inspiration for *Smiles* came when she was a little closer to home—at the dentist's office, to be exact! Whether she's been traveling to exciting locales or merely visiting the dentist, Cathie is always glad to get back home to her two cats, her trusty word processor and her hidden cache of Oreo cookies!

One

Wham! Laura Peters had been running, trying to get out of the pouring rain, when she abruptly plowed into an immovable object. *A brick wall, perhaps?* she wondered hazily. *One that grunted?*

The grunt, plus a muttered curse, made Laura realize she'd rammed into a man who just happened to be built like a brick wall. In his favor was the fact that he also happened to have a pair of warm hands, which were currently cupping her elbows, steadying her as she blinked the raindrops out of her eyes. Now if she could catch her breath, she'd be fine.

At least she was temporarily out of the blinding downpour, Laura reminded herself. The storm had caught her totally by surprise. But then so had this man.

"Sorry," she gasped once she had enough air to speak. "I . . . didn't see . . . you."

"That's reassuring," he noted in a teasing voice. "I wasn't sure if you were on a suicidal mission or what."

"I was trying to get out of the rain. Getting under this awning seemed like a good idea."

"It was a good idea. Running head-on into me..." He shook his head. "Now *that* was a questionable call. Are you okay?" he asked belatedly.

Laura nodded and tried to disregard the tiny shivers running up and down her spine. Granted it was cool outside; after all, it was only March and this was Massachusetts. But these shivers were *warm*, and they seemed to originate from where he was holding her. Which was silly, of course. His touch was polite; not intimate, not threatening. But courtesy had never felt like this before, she noted somewhat uneasily.

"I've gotta tell you, you pack quite a wallop, lady!" he informed her wryly.

"So do you," she replied as she stepped away from him.

Shoving her wet hair out of her eyes, she attempted to sneak a peek at her fellow refugee from the storm. At five foot seven she was tall, but he was taller, although not by much. His dark hair was a little on the long side and had a tendency to curl. His warm brown eyes were "full of the devil," as her mother used to say. And he had a smile to match.

Unlike her, he was more appropriately dressed for the weather. His feet were protected by a pair of construction boots while hers were stuck in soggy leather pumps. His jeans showed no effect from the rain while her raw silk slacks were now mottled with wet patches. He wore a nylon jacket that protected him from the rain. Unfortunately her own classic navy blazer hadn't done a thing to protect her or her expensive white blouse, which was now clinging to her like a second skin.

Catching the way he was looking at her, she hurriedly glanced down to make sure that said blouse hadn't been transformed by the rain into a see-through come-on. To her relief, all was well but she buttoned up her blazer just in case.

"A little late for that, isn't it?" the man said in amusement.

"Late for what?" she asked in a cool voice intended to mask her discomfiture.

"Late to be buttoning up against the rain. You're already soaking wet. Come on, I think it's a little drier back here." He led her away from the dripping awning and closer to the building's protected entryway. "There, that's better."

Better? she repeated silently. *Sure it was drier, but it was also... Riskier.* There was just something about being stranded together in such close quarters that created an unexpected impression of intimacy. The sheets of rain formed a curtain that kept them in—and the rest of the world out.

Seclusion. Protection. The feelings were there, helped along by the simple fact that she and her fellow refugee were standing so close that Laura could practically feel him breathing. There wasn't much room, and what space there was seemed to be shrinking by the second.

Laura told herself she wasn't uncomfortable. She told herself she was imagining things. She told herself she wasn't the type to go all weak-kneed just because she was standing next to a man in a deserted doorway.

The talking-to didn't do much good.

So she stuck her hands in her pockets—a sure sign that she was nervous but trying to hide it—and attempted to initiate a polite conversation. Anything to break this heavy provocative silence that was growing between them.

"The forecast said it would be clear and sunny today."

"Everyone knew it would rain today," the man replied with utter confidence. "Ralph's bunions were acting up yesterday. Sure sign that rain was coming."

Laura frowned in confusion. "Who's Ralph?"

"Not from around here, are you?"

"I certainly am from around here," she retorted. "Not originally, perhaps, but I've lived here in Baileys Crossing for almost three years now." Coming from the urban jungle of Chicago, Laura had grown very fond of the charming perfection of the small New England town.

"Three years?" The man shook his head. "And you don't know about Ralph and his bunions? Amazing. He owns Ralph's Hardware and Feed Store. And his weather predictions are more accurate than the National Weather Service any day. Everyone in town knows that."

"Fine," she said tartly, stung by his insinuation that she was unknowledgeable. "Next time I plan on going out for a walk, I'll check with Ralph first."

"You do that."

Silence fell again. She could feel his eyes on her, could see the way his gaze lingered on her face, her lips. Then he smiled, which made her even more uneasy. It was the kind of smile that said, *I know more about you than you know about yourself.* She shifted restlessly and inadvertently brushed her arm against his.

Time to try polite conversation again, she decided. "Too bad it's Sunday and all the stores are closed," she said brightly. "Otherwise we could just step inside instead of staying out here."

"You shop here often?" he asked.

Something in his voice, a certain note of masculine speculation, made Laura suspicious. She had good reason to be. Looking over her shoulder, she saw the display window for Lilly's, the finest lingerie store in Baileys Crossing—the *only* lingerie store in Baileys Crossing. As if that wasn't bad enough, Lilly had chosen to display two of her sexiest nightgowns in the window, along with a white silk chemise and tap pants set exactly like the set Laura just happened to be wearing under her wet clothes.

"Shop here?" Laura shook her head vehemently and dug her hands deeper into her pockets. "Never." It wasn't the truth, of course, but somehow preventing further speculation on his part was more important than being totally honest.

"Never?"

She stuck to her guns. "Never."

"Too bad. That one looks nice, doesn't it?" He pointed to the ice-blue nightgown that was more lace than nightgown.

She shrugged.

"You'd look good in something like that."

"No, I wouldn't!"

"Well, you'd certainly look better in it than I would," he maintained.

She looked away from the laughter in his brown eyes. She suddenly felt warm all over. It was not just embarrassment; she felt a disturbing amount of awareness, as well. Deciding to play it safe, she moved a little farther from him and a little closer to escape.

"I'm sorry," the man said softly. "I didn't mean to make you feel uncomfortable. Maybe we should introduce ourselves." He held out his hand. "I'm Sam Mitchell."

She gave him and his hand a wary look before participating in the handshake.

"And you are?" he prompted her.

She looked into his eyes and made the decision. "Leaving. The rain's let up. Nice meeting you, Mr. Mitchell. Goodbye."

"Wait a second!" he called after her. "What's your name?"

"Laura."

"Laura what?"

"Just Laura."

"I'm telling you, she was beautiful," Sam Mitchell said to his brother Frank a few days later. The two of them shared an office at the family business of Mitchell and Sons, Architectural Salvagers. "Even dripping wet. Her hair was blond, I think, although it looked darker when it was wet. And she had the biggest brown eyes you ever saw. She was sort of haughty, but cute."

"Cute?" Frank repeated in amazement. "You've never gone for cute before."

"Beautiful," Sam corrected. "She was beautiful. But she took off before I could get her full name. I've been asking everyone I can think of if they know her. Her name's Laura."

"I know. You've told me so at least two dozen times since you met her."

"I've got to find her again," Sam declared.

"How come?"

"How come?" Sam repeated. "Because I liked her."

"You've liked a lot of brown-eyed blondes. Some green-eyed redheads, too. And a few—"

"Get out of here." Sam scrunched up a blank work order and tossed it at his brother. "There haven't been that many women in my life."

After ducking, Frank shrugged. "All I know is that between you, me and Joey, you're the only one who hasn't gotten married."

"I'm in no hurry," Sam said as he settled more comfortably into his old-fashioned leather office chair.

"Yeah, Mom's noticed that."

"Her oldest and her youngest sons are married and she's already got grandchildren—she should be happy with that."

"Try telling Mom that," Frank suggested.

"I have," Sam retorted. "*Many* times."

The sound of the phone ringing interrupted their discussion. It was Frank's line.

Sam was plotting additional ways of tracking Laura down when he looked up and noticed that Frank's face was pale.

Sam was out of his chair in an instant. "What is it?" he asked. "What's wrong?"

"That was my mother-in-law. Anne's in labor. I've gotta go to the hospital." Frank put the phone in his out basket and then grabbed Sam by the shirtfront. "The baby's not due for another two weeks!" he said frantically.

"Calm down." Sam carefully released himself from his brother's stranglehold. "Remember when Cindy was born? She was almost two weeks early and there was no problem. Babies have got their own time schedule. You should know that by now."

"Oh, no!" Frank smacked the heel of his hand against his forehead. "Cindy! I almost forgot. I was supposed to pick her up from kindergarten and take her to the dentist today." He pointed to Sam. "You'll have to do it."

Sam's stomach dropped to his shoes. "Me?"

"You."

Sam hated dentists. It was nothing personal; he just had a natural aversion to pain. He didn't have many weaknesses, God knew, but going to the dentist's office was definitely one of them.

Unfortunately Sam couldn't see any way of avoiding it. His younger brother, Joey, was out with the flu, as was Joey's wife, and his parents were vacationing in Florida. Meanwhile Frank was clearly needed at the hospital. Which left him . . . on his way to the dentist's office, he concluded resignedly. It wasn't exactly the way he'd anticipated spending his afternoon.

"When's Cindy's appointment?" Sam remembered to ask as Frank flew out the door.

"Forty-five minutes. You'd better hurry."

Hurry? To a dentist's office? Frank had to be kidding! "Yeah, right. Thanks, bro. I owe you one," Sam muttered to his brother's rapidly retreating back.

He then sat down just as Mabel, the woman who'd been the secretary at Mitchell and Sons since day one, passed by. "Hey, Mabel, wait up a second." When the stout woman stopped in the doorway, Sam flashed her a cocky smile. "I've got a special assignment for you this afternoon."

"No, I'm not taking Cindy to the dentist for you," she retorted with the bluntness of a woman who'd had her job longer than he'd been alive. "Frank said you're doing it."

"But Mabel, think of that poor little girl facing that terrible dentist's office, alone . . . scared."

"She won't be alone, you'll be with her. And she won't be scared for long, you'll make sure of that."

Sam sighed. "You're a hard-hearted woman, Mabel."

"Yeah, I know. That's why I've lasted this long around here. Now stop bothering me so I can reschedule your appointments for this afternoon."

"Tell MacNamara I'll tour the old Tandy place first thing in the morning. Remind him that the workmen aren't to touch a thing until I get there and decide which pieces are to be salvaged."

"To look at that broken-down old house you'd never guess that there was anything to salvage inside," Mabel noted. "It's been empty for almost a decade. The place is practically falling down."

"Ah, but finding the valuable pieces hiding beneath all the junk is my job, Mabel."

"And you're damn good at it," Mabel admitted. "Your father planned well when he raised you three boys to take over the business."

Sam wasn't sure how much was due to planning and how much was a result of simple necessity. He'd certainly never planned on joining the family business. His plans had involved going to college, maybe becoming an architect. But things hadn't worked out that way. He didn't have any regrets; he seldom had time for them. Besides, he probably wasn't college material anyway—unlike his older brother, Frank.

Mabel rested one hip against the door frame. "Yep," she went on, "you always were the perfect choice to do the scouting work."

"It's called acquisitions, Mabel."

"Call it whatever you want, I like scouting. Suits you better. Makes you sound like a character from one of my Louis L'Amour westerns. The scouting renegade. You always were the renegade in the family. The happy-go-lucky one."

"Not very happy at the moment, Mabel. But you could change that. Sure you don't want to take Cindy to the dentist?"

"Positive."

And so it was that half an hour later Sam found himself riding the medical building's elevator to Dr. Peters's second-floor office, with niece Cindy in hand. He would have preferred taking the stairs, but five-year-old Cindy loved elevators. Looking down at the smiling little girl, he wondered when the tears and panic would set in. The kid was going to the dentist. Didn't she realize that? He sure did. He wasn't even aware that he was grimacing until Cindy squeezed his hand and said, "'Sokay, Uncle Sam. Me and Dr. Peters are friends."

He couldn't seem to come up with an answer to that, so he tried to smile but had a feeling he didn't do a very good job of it.

The dentist's office surprised him. The reception area was large and airy. The walls were covered with pictures of Disney Characters, such as Mickey Mouse, and half the furniture was scaled down to kid-size. It didn't bear much resemblance to a torture chamber, but then appearances could be deceiving.

The receptionist, a woman in her early fifties, gave Sam a welcoming smile. He thought she looked familiar, but he wasn't exactly in the clearest frame of mind. All he wanted to do was get in and out as quickly as possible.

"Mitchell," he said curtly. "One o'clock appointment. How long's the wait?"

"Dr. Peters is running right on time," the receptionist said. "We're ready for Cindy now."

That sounded ominous. Sam looked down at the innocently trusting little face turned up to his. He swallowed. "You want me to come in with you, small fry?" he asked her gruffly.

Cindy shook her head so vehemently her pigtails flew. "I'm a big girl now! I can go in by myself."

"Then I'll wait right out here for you, okay?"

Cindy nodded.

Sam sat down and waited. And waited. He impatiently checked his watch. Had it been only five minutes? Impossible. It felt like twenty. He picked up a magazine, then tossed it down. Was that a drill he heard? He got up and started pacing. The other adults in the waiting room, two moms, looked at him as if he were nuts, but Sam didn't care. What the hell were they doing to his little niece?

He soon lost whatever patience he'd had. "How much longer is it going to take?" he demanded of the receptionist.

"Cindy's just here for a checkup. It won't be much longer now."

Sam sweated every remaining second until he heard the sweet sound of Cindy's voice. "Are you okay?" he asked, rushing over to meet the little girl as she came through the door. He crouched down low so that he could look into Cindy's eyes, searching for tears.

"Are you the anxious father?" a husky voice asked.

"No, I—" Sam looked up and couldn't believe his eyes. "You!" He quickly stood up. He'd found her. Laura!

Two

Sam couldn't believe his luck. It had to be fate, and he fully intended to make the most of it. This time he had no intention of letting Laura get away so easily.

"So we meet again," Sam murmured. "I've been looking for you."

"You have?" Laura was on her own turf now, and she felt much more confident than she had the last time they'd met. "Why?"

"We never finished our discussion."

"I don't recall any discussion," she said.

"Guess I'll have to jog your memory a little. We were talking about whether or not you'd look good in that little blue number in Lilly's window, remember?"

Laura wanted to sink through the floor. It didn't help any that the two women sitting in the far corner of the waiting room were watching her and Sam with avid interest. She was just glad that Sam had spoken quietly enough that no one else could hear what he'd said. "You're imagining things, Mr. Mitchell," she retorted briskly, stepping back into the inner office. "Now, as I was saying, there was no need for you to be concerned. Your daughter didn't have any cavities at all."

"Daughter?" Sam frowned, following her. "I don't have a daughter."

"But I thought Cindy..."

"This squirt?" He reached down to tug one of Cindy's pigtails. "Naw, she's not my daughter."

"Uncle Sam isn't anybody's daddy," Cindy piped up. "He's just a bachelor."

Just a bachelor too sure of his own offbeat charm, Laura thought to herself. "I see."

"So you work here, huh?" Sam asked.

Laura nodded.

"Cindy tells me that this Dr. Peters isn't such an ogre after all," he said. "You must enjoy working with him."

Cindy tugged on his hand. "But, Uncle Sam—"

"Not now, Cindy." He patted his niece on the head while keeping his eyes on Laura. "So what are you, the dental hygienist or something?"

"Uncle Sam—"

"Later, small fry. I like the white coat, Laura. Not as much as I liked that blue nightgown, but it's not bad. So tell me, what are you doing working in a dental office? You enjoy working with this guy, Dr. Peters?"

Laura smiled at the prospect of watching Sam Mitchell put his foot in his mouth. "Dr. Peters is great."

"Great at what? Inflicting pain?"

"Do I detect a bad attitude toward dentists?" Laura inquired.

"You sure do," he readily confirmed.

"You don't like dentists?"

"Who does?"

"I do," Cindy said. "I like Dr. Peters."

"I know you do, small fry. And that's fine. Just give me a minute to talk to this beautiful lady here and convince her to go out to dinner with me tonight."

Cindy shook her head. "I don't think that's gonna work, Uncle Sam."

"Thanks for the vote of confidence, squirt."

"I'd listen to your niece if I were you, Mr. Mitchell," Laura suggested.

"The name's Sam. And why should I listen to Cindy?"

"Because you don't like dentists," Laura replied. "Now call me unreasonable, but I don't go out with men who don't like me."

"I didn't say I didn't like you. I said—" He broke off. "Wait a minute. You mean you're . . . ?"

She nodded. "You got it. I'm Dr. Laura Peters."

"Oops."

Much to her surprise, and chagrin, Laura felt her lips lifting into a reluctant smile. She'd never heard a grown man say oops before. It was rather endearing. At least it was when Sam Mitchell said it. But then he'd been having an unusual effect on her since the moment she'd first bumped into him.

"I tried to tell you, Uncle Sam," Cindy said.

"So you did, small fry. Next time remind me to listen to you," he noted ruefully. "You're really a dentist?" he asked Laura.

"That's what it says on my degree."

Sam shook his head in amazement. "You don't look like any dentist I've ever met."

"Have you met many?"

"More than my fair share. And none of them had legs like yours."

She sighed. "Are you always this outrageous or is this just for my benefit?"

He grinned at her. "Hey, I'm on my best behavior."

"In that case I'd hate to see your worst."

"How bad can I, lifelong resident of Baileys Crossing, be?"

"I don't know," Laura retorted, "and I don't aim on finding out."

"Ah, but that's what makes life fun—the things we *don't* aim on finding out, the things that hit us anyway. The ones that catch you off guard and knock you off your feet. It can happen anytime, anyplace. You could be standing somewhere, minding your own business on a rainy Sunday afternoon, when suddenly, out of nowhere, comes this madwoman—"

"Madwoman!" Laura protested.

"Who practically knocks me off my feet. Like Prince Charming I go searching the realm looking for this lady. Keep in mind that I don't even have a glass slipper to go by. All I've got is a name. Laura. Then, just as I was about to despair of ever finding her—"

"You don't look like the despairing type to me," Laura inserted dryly.

"—fate steps in and arranges for us to meet again."

"This is all fascinating, I'm sure, but I've got other patients to see."

"Sure, I understand," he said agreeably. "Just tell me what time to pick you up and I'll be out of here."

Laura frowned. "Pick me up?"

"For dinner tonight. Do you prefer seafood or steak?"

"I don't recall you asking me to go out for dinner—"

"Consider yourself asked," he said.

"Consider yourself refused," she retorted. Then, because she felt guilty at being so curt with him, she elaborated further. "Look, I've got office hours until eight tonight, but even if I didn't, I don't think going out to dinner with you is a good idea."

"Good ideas are rarely the best ones to follow through on. Don't you know that?"

"No, I don't know that. What I do know is that I've got other patients to see." Laura deliberately shifted her attention from Sam to his young niece. "Goodbye, Cindy. And congratulations on that new baby brother or sister of yours. You must be excited about that."

"Not really," Cindy said glumly. "I'd much rather have a kitten. That's what I *really* wanted."

"We can't always have what we want," Laura stated automatically.

"Why not?" the little girl asked.

"Good question," Sam said, his look a clear challenge to Laura.

Why not? Laura repeated silently. She certainly didn't know the answer to that one. She only knew that life seemed to work out that way. "I'll let your uncle explain it to you. Goodbye, Cindy." She retreated to the sanctum of an examining room with relief. She could handle fractious children and their anxious parents with no problem, but flirtatious men were a little out of her field.

It was rather disconcerting to discover she was susceptible to Sam Mitchell's particular brand of charm. Hopefully the symptoms would wear off with time. She'd give herself two minutes. Then she'd start to worry.

Out in the waiting room Cindy was looking up at Sam. "Well, Uncle Sam, how come I can't have what I want?"

He shrugged. "Beats me, squirt. Who knows? Maybe you'll get a kitten *and* a baby brother or sister."

Cindy's entire face lighted up. "Think so?"

"Anything's possible." Anything, Sam thought, including him getting what he wanted . . . Laura Peters. Now if he could just get used to thinking of her as a dentist.

Sam shook his head. First he had to get out of this office. That damn drill was whining again, preventing him from thinking straight. Or was Laura the one responsible for his muddled thinking? Her smile, her big brown eyes, her shapely legs—any one of the above was enough to cloud a man's thoughts. Add her beautiful blond hair, luscious mouth and cool silky voice, and it was no wonder that he felt as if he'd been hit with a sledgehammer.

Then again, he reminded himself with self-derision, it could simply be the smell of antiseptic and the sound of a dental drill having an adverse effect on him. Either way it was time for him to make a quick getaway and regroup.

"I have not yet begun to fight," he muttered as he grabbed Cindy's hand and rushed her out of the office.

"'Sokay, Uncle Sam," Cindy said. "I won't tell anyone you're scared of dentists. It'll be our secret."

"Thanks, squirt. At this point I can use all the help I can get. Tell me, how long have you been going to Dr. Peters?" And so the pursuit began.

"All right, Hazel, tell me everything you know about Sam Mitchell," Laura asked her receptionist when they had a break later that afternoon. The two minutes she'd allotted herself to recover from Sam's visit were long since over, and she was still curious.

"Which do you want—the long or the condensed version?"

Laura consulted her watch before answering. "Condensed for now. I've got another patient in a few minutes."

"Okay, here it goes. Sam Mitchell. Born on July first, thirty-four years ago. Never been married but has two brothers—one older, one younger—who are married. He works in the family business, Mitchell and Sons, which does architectural salvaging. Never been in trouble with the law, has dented a few hearts but is careful not to break them and

is good with kids and animals—although he'd be the last one
to tell you so himself. Pays his bills on time, drives an old
Mustang and, judging from his crabby behavior when he
walked in here, is not at ease in a dental office. Usually he's
quite a charmer, very popular with the ladies in town. *All*
the ladies. From five to ninety-five. It's that sense of humor of his, you see, plus that grin.''

"You're amazing," Laura said in admiration. "And
that's just the condensed version? I'm impressed."

"In a small town like this it isn't hard keeping track of
people. The Mitchells have lived in Baileys Crossing for
generations."

"Sam really has lived here all his life then?" Laura had
wondered if that had been a line of his.

Hazel nodded. "There was talk of him leaving to explore
the world, but his dad's health took a turn for the worse at
about that time and Sam was needed at home. He pitched
in to keep ·Mitchell and Sons running." She frowned,
thinking hard. "Let's see, Sam must have been about nineteen then. His older brother was twenty-two and young Joey
would only have been about thirteen. Luckily their dad re-
covered, but Mr. Mitchell needed his sons' help, so the boys
continued to work there until they eventually took over.
Now I can't imagine Sam ever leaving Baileys Crossing.
Funny, isn't it, how things work out."

"Yeah, funny." Laura knew from her own experience
that life could take some unexpected turns. The problem was
learning how to cope, with the high expectations and new
responsibilities. It was something she was still trying to do.

Hazel reclaimed her attention by waving a pink message
slip in the air. "Not to change the subject, but I meant to tell
you that Dr. Morley called and said he'd be in at five-thirty
instead of six."

Laura's mind was now completely back on business.
"Good. Then I can talk to him before he starts seeing pa-

tients." There were a number of business matters that she needed to discuss with Jerry Morley, her friend and partner. Their practice, with Jerry doing general dentistry while she specialized in children's dentistry, was flourishing. They had met at dental school, and their friendship had eventually led to Jerry's invitation to join him in Baileys Crossing, in the practice he'd inherited from his father.

"Let's see, what else was there?" Hazel checked her notes. "Oh, yes. I also meant to ask you about these two accounts." She pulled two folders from the corner of her desk. "Susan Weisman's delinquent in her payments. And I had a question on the Chos' account. Did you mean to charge them only half the going rate?"

Laura nodded. "Mr Cho is out of work right now. They're having a tough time of it. And Susan Weisman is going through a divorce. She'll pay as soon as she gets the settlement. Her daughter was one of my first patients. She's good for it."

"That she is," Hazel agreed. "That answers my questions, I guess. Did I answer all yours about Sam Mitchell?"

"You certainly did. Thanks."

"He's a hard man to ignore, but I suspect you'll find that out for yourself," Hazel predicted.

Even though Sam continued to remain stubbornly in Laura's thoughts as she left the office that evening, it was still something of a surprise to find him waiting for her in the parking lot next to the building.

"What are you doing out here in the dark?" she asked. "It's cold out here."

He shrugged and tucked his hands farther into his pockets. His shoulders were already hunched against the cold, making him look as if he were carrying the weight of the world.

Laura frowned. Granted she hadn't known Sam very long, but she could tell that something was very wrong.

"Sam, are you okay?"

"It's a boy."

It took her a moment to make sense of his statement. "Your brother's baby is a boy?"

Sam nodded. "But there were complications." His voice was completely flat. "The baby is in an incubator. Something's wrong...I don't know what. And I don't know what I'm doing here dumping on you. It's not your problem. Forget it." He turned as if to leave.

"No, wait a second. I'm sorry to hear that the baby is in an incubator, but maybe it's not as bad as you think. What did the doctor actually say?'

"What do doctors ever say?" he retorted angrily. "That we'd have to wait and see what happened. And then he added a bunch of that technical jargon doctors use when they don't want you to know what's really going on." Stopping to take a deep breath, Sam looked away from her. "I'm no good at this sort of thing," he admitted in a quiet voice. "I had to get out of that hospital, so I got in the car and just started driving. Next thing I knew, I ended up here." He shrugged.

"How long has it been since you checked in with the hospital?"

He looked at his watch and noted the time with some surprise. "It's been two hours."

"Come on, let's go inside and give them a call. Maybe things have improved by now."

When Sam showed no sign of moving, Laura took him by the arm and tugged gently. "Come on," she repeated, "let's go inside for a minute."

He came quietly, a sure sign that he wasn't himself.

They met Jerry on their way into the office. "What are you doing back here?" he asked Laura. "I thought you'd left."

"I decided to come back. You can go on home, Jerry. I'll lock up."

Jerry cast a curious look at Sam. "Hi, Sam. What are you doing here?"

"I'll explain some other time," Laura stated, on Sam's behalf.

Jerry left reluctantly.

As soon as he'd done so, Laura placed the call to the area hospital for Sam and then handed him the phone. She watched him closely, trying to gauge what was going on by his expression. To her relief, his features seemed to relax.

"The baby's doing better?" he said into the phone. "You're sure? Is my brother there? Yeah, that's right. The one who's been grabbing the doctors by their shirtfronts. Sure, I'll hold." Sam closed his eyes and took a deep breath.

Laura noticed that his voice was much lighter when he spoke to his brother. "Hey, bro, how are you holding up? Good. Yeah, well, the nurse said the baby is doing better, but what did the doctor say? Out of the woods? He said that? Before or after you strong-armed him? You kissed him? Listen, Frank, I wouldn't make a habit of that. Yeah, I know, I know. It is a big relief. No, I didn't call Mom and Pop. I told you I wouldn't without your approval. Yeah, right, why put them through the stress. Sure, we're tough. We can handle this stuff no problem. Cindy? I left her with the neighbors, just like you said. Yeah, she and her girl-friend were playing when I left. Don't worry about it, I'll keep tabs on things at this end. You just take care of Anne and that new baby of yours. Yeah, me too, bro. See ya.

"They're gonna be okay," Sam said after hanging up.

"I'm glad," Laura replied softly.

"I feel like a real idiot," he confessed.

"Why?"

"Getting all upset that way. Coming here and dumping it all on you."

"*That's* no reason to feel like an idiot. I can think of several much better reasons for you to feel that way," she teased, hoping to make him feel more at ease.

Sam raised his brows. "You wouldn't by any chance be referring to my valiant attempt to ask you out, now would you?"

"Actually, I was thinking more along the lines of your chauvinistic assumption that I was the dental hygienist."

"Oh, that."

"Yes, that."

"I guess you could say today has just been one of those days. A real bi—" He broke off. "A real bad day. You know, when Frank asked me to take Cindy to the dentist for him, I was not pleased. In fact, I made a big deal out of it. Stupid of me." Sam looked around the empty office and grimaced. "But then as you already know, dental offices are not my favorite hangouts."

"I've gotten that impression, yes. And now I'm getting the impression that you're feeling guilty about not wanting to bring Cindy here in the first place." Laura was an expert in guilt; she'd certainly experienced it enough times herself to recognize it in others. "Am I right?"

Sam shrugged. "I didn't exactly jump up and volunteer for the job. And I should have."

"The bottom line, though, is that you did help your brother, complaints or not, and everything's going to be okay."

"My brother helped me, too, you know." Ever so gently, Sam brushed the back of his hand against her cheek. "He led me to you."

Laura felt as though the rug had been yanked out from under her. She and Sam had been discussing things person to person. Now suddenly it was man to woman.

One touch and she felt the return of the overwhelming awareness she'd experienced the first time she'd run into him. It was even more powerful now, and just as disturbing.

"Ah, well, um, it's getting late."

Sam sighed at her retreat. "I did it again, didn't I? Scared you off. I seem to be getting real good at that. And it's not exactly something I want to be good at with you," he murmured meaningfully. "I had something else in mind."

"I'll bet you did." He'd certainly made the jump from vulnerable family man to Don Juan fast enough, she decided crossly.

"I could just as easily be scared off by you, you know," he informed her. "I mean, here I am, alone in a dental office filled with instruments of torture, at the complete mercy of a beautiful dentist. Who knows what you might do to me?"

His look of horrified anticipation was irresistible. Before she knew it, her lips were curving upward. She shook her head in amazement. "Why is it that you're able to make me smile right when I'm about to get angry with you?"

"Talent. Sheer talent. Besides, I like your smile. It's cute."

"Cute?" she repeated in astonishment.

"Don't say it like it's a four-letter word," he reprimanded her. "It's a compliment."

Laura shook her head. "I'm thirty-one. That's a little old to be called cute."

"You're younger than I am, and I'm still cute, so that argument holds no water with me, kid."

Laura couldn't help it. She cracked up.

"Your laugh's not bad, either," he added.

"Aren't you going to tell me it's something I should do more often?"

Sam shook his head. "I wouldn't dream of saying such a thing. Then you'd be sure not to laugh just to be stubborn."

"What makes you think you know so much about me?"

"Just my native intelligence, I guess. I mean, Baileys Crossing may be small, but its lifelong residents aren't dumb."

"Just tactless on occasion?"

He grinned. "Okay, I'll accept tactless. So how about letting me make it up to you by taking you out to dinner?"

"I already ate dinner at the office."

"How about grabbing a cup of coffee at the B.C. Café, then?" When she hesitated, he said, "Look, it's the least I can do to repay your taking me in and offering me the use of your phone. And frankly I could use the company. How about you?"

"A cup of coffee sounds good," she had to admit. She made no reference to his company, but the prospect of sharing some of that didn't sound too bad, either.

Once they got to the small restaurant, which was right around the corner, there was no resisting the tempting smell of freshly baked pie. One sniff and Sam was able to identify it as French apple.

"How do you know that?" Laura asked.

"I read it on the blackboard up there."

She looked, and sure enough, written in pink flowery script were the words Home-Baked Pies: Today's Special— French Apple.

"Clever."

"I've always thought so," he agreed with a grin. "How about a slice to go with your coffee?"

"It has possibilities."

"Ah, possibilities! Now there's a subject worth discussing." But before he could do so, they were joined by the teenage waitress who'd come to seat them. "Hi, Judy," he greeted her. "How's that basketball-playing brother of yours?"

"He's doing fine, Sam. He's settling in at Boston College just like you said he would."

"Glad to hear it."

"Did you ever find that Laura you were looking for?" Judy asked him.

"Sure did. Right here. Dr. Laura Peters, Judy Reilly."

"Gosh, I had no idea Dr. Peters was the Laura you were looking for. She comes in here for lunch a couple times a week. I never knew your first name was Laura. She's a dentist, you know," Judy added for Sam's benefit.

"I know," he replied. "I found that out today."

"What a surprise. Gosh."

After Judy had taken their order, Laura made an observation. "Now *she's* cute."

"Judy? She's just a kid."

"She's sixteen if she's a day. And she likes you."

"Sure she does. So do her mother and her grandmother. I'm a very likable guy."

Laura shook her head. "Have you always had this effect on women?"

"What effect? The ability to make them smile, to make them laugh? Yeah, it's a tough job but somebody's got to do it."

"I can tell you're suffering," she retorted wryly.

"How about you? Have you always had this effect on men?"

"What effect?" she asked.

"Knocking them off their feet."

"No, I don't make a habit of doing that."

"Good," Sam said. "I'm glad to hear it."

"You seem to have a strange idea of what I'm really like. I'm hardly the femme fatale type."

"What type do you think you are?" he asked.

"The hardworking, serious type. Why? What type do you think I am?"

"*My* type."

Three

———

"Can I get you two anything else?" their waitress asked in what Laura felt was an extremely timely interruption.

"I'll have another cup of coffee," Sam said, then glanced at Laura. "What about you?"

"No, thanks. I'm fine." But the truth was that she wasn't fine at all. In fact, she was feeling nervous and decidedly unsettled.

Sam's comment about her being his type had thrown her. He'd only been teasing, of course. He didn't even know her. But then no one *really* knew her. She didn't let them. They had their own image of her—cool, classy, confident—and she let them keep that image. It had nothing to do with the reality of her life.

The facts were simple and not unique. No money meant hard times. Laura had been only four when her father had died and her mother had had to go out to work. They'd moved in with her mother's sister, a widow with a three-year-old daughter of her own.

Hard times had gotten harder as her mother, who was ill prepared for the job of being sole provider, had valiantly struggled to keep food on the table and a roof over their heads. Laura ended up being raised as much by her aunt as by her mother. Rules were set and strictly adhered to. She could still remember some of them....

Rule #1: *Eat everything on your plate.* Some days that was harder to do than others. Those were the days—and there were plenty of them—when dinner had consisted of stewed tomatoes: on bread, on noodles, on spaghetti, on instant mashed potatoes, on anything that didn't move. To this day Laura couldn't stand to look at, let alone eat, stewed tomatoes.

Rule #2: *No TV until homework is done.* Since the tiny black-and-white TV was broken more frequently than it worked, this wasn't usually an issue.

Rule #3: *No new clothes.* Laura and her cousin, April, had shared hand-me-downs obtained from church rummage sales and made wearable again by her aunt's skill with a needle. Laura had been nineteen before she'd ever gotten a new dress of her own, and that one had been marked down by half. She still had it folded away somewhere.

Laura closed her eyes. They'd lived hand to mouth for so long that even now she had a difficult time accepting that those tough days in Chicago were over. She knew her cousin, April, felt the same way.

"You're a million miles away," Sam murmured, wondering what had brought such a melancholy look to her face.

"Sorry about that." She opened her eyes and smiled. "You were saying?"

"That you were my type. And you were going to say...?" he prompted her.

"That they bake a very good apple pie here," she stated firmly.

Sam acknowledged her complete change of subject with a wry smile. "I can't argue with that."

"Good." She took a sip of coffee, grimacing as she realized she'd forgotten to add cream. "I don't like arguing."

"No? I'll try to keep that in mind. How about talking about yourself? Do you like doing that?"

She shifted in her seat. "Not really."

"Does that mean I'll have to pry information out of you?"

"That depends on what you want to know," she said warily.

"Let's start with the simple stuff. You already mentioned that you've lived here almost three years—which I find hard to believe, by the way."

"Why?"

"Because our paths haven't crossed before this," he replied. "Baileys Crossing isn't exactly huge."

"That's one of the reasons why I like it," Laura admitted. "It's large enough to have everything you need, but small enough to be cozy."

Now they were getting somewhere, Sam thought. "So...you like cozy, huh?"

"On occasion."

"Really? On *which* occasions?" he immediately asked.

"Christmas and New Year's," she retorted, knowing exactly where his thoughts were headed. "Are you ever serious?" she demanded in exasperation.

"On Christmas and New Year's," he promptly retorted.

Laura smiled before she could stop herself. She shook her head. "You know, Hazel warned me about you."

"I find that hard to believe."

"She did. She told me you were very popular with the ladies. She said it was your grin and your sense of humor."

"That was nice of her. That bribe I gave her to say something good about me worked, I guess."

"Hazel's unbribable."

"How about Jerry? Is he unbribable, too?" Sam asked.

"He's my partner. And yes, I'd say he's unbribable, too."

"Is he *just* your partner?"

Laura didn't know how to respond to that question. Not because she didn't know the answer; she did. But she didn't know if she wanted to tell Sam. It would only spur him on to ask more questions. Not that he needed much prompting, she noted wryly.

In the end she simply stuck to the truth. "He's my friend as well as my business partner."

"*Just* friends?"

"Just friends. His wife prefers it that way," she noted dryly, "and so do I."

"Any other partners, business or otherwise, waiting in the wings?"

"None that I intend telling you about."

"Which means no," Sam translated. "Good."

Annoyed by his satisfied expression, Laura said, "How did we get started on this subject anyway?"

"I said you were my type."

"Me and half of Baileys Crossing, right?"

"No, just you."

Laura didn't mean to look at him. But somehow her eyes moved to his and the next thing she knew she was caught—entangled. His gaze held hers, and she felt as if he'd touched her very soul. With effort she broke the eye contact, but not the spell he seemed to have cast over her.

She tartly reminded herself to wake up and smell the coffee. Sam probably looked at half the female population of Baileys Crossing that way. So calm down, and change the subject.

"It must have been nice growing up in a town like this."

"Nice enough," he agreed. "How about you? Where did you grow up?"

"Chicago. But now I live in one of those large Victorian houses that have been converted into town houses," she went on to say. *Great. Tell him exactly where you live, why don't you?* She couldn't help it, she excused herself. The memories of those bleak years in Chicago made her so uneasy, she was rarely willing to talk about them.

"Large Victorian houses..." Sam repeated thoughtfully. "You mean those town houses over on Elm Street?"

Laura gave up. It was a small town after all. He'd have no trouble finding out where she lived if he really wanted to know. "Right."

"We provided a lot of the materials for that project. My family's in the architectural salvaging business, in case you didn't know."

"Actually, I did know that," she took pleasure in saying.

"Hazel, right?"

Laura nodded. Since she didn't actually know what architectural salvaging was, she asked him.

"It means we take pieces of buildings that are scheduled for demolition and we store them, reselling them to builders and renovators for projects like your town house renovation. The quality of the material and the workmanship from that time—on things like millwork, staircases, woodwork or mantelpieces—can't be recreated today. My job is to find those pieces from what was once a fine building before it all becomes a pile of rubble. My secretary calls it scouting. We call it acquisition work."

"It sounds fascinating. You must know a lot about the architectural history of each building to know what's good and what's not."

"It was more a matter of learning on the job. My dad taught me a lot."

"Do your parents live here in Baileys Crossing, too?"

Sam nodded. "They're on vacation down in Florida now, though. Aren't due back until the end of next week. Pop's blood pressure has been getting kind of high lately, and the doctor ordered that he have some rest. Getting him out of the state was the only way to make sure of that. Frank's going to call them tonight and give them a watered-down version of the delivery. But enough about my family. What about yours?"

Here it was again, that lump in her throat that came whenever anyone asked her about her past. She tried to keep her reply brief, relating only the facts because the emotions still hurt too much. "I don't have much family left anymore. My father died when I was very young. I was raised by my mother and my aunt. They sort of shared the job until they were both killed in a car accident. That happened ten years ago," she said quietly. "Now there's just my cousin and me. We grew up together. She owns a restaurant in Michigan."

"I'm sorry. About the loss of the rest of your family, I mean."

So was she, but that was something else Laura had a hard time dealing with. Her mother and her aunt had died the day before Laura had graduated from college—their car had crashed while they were driving down to see her at the University of Illinois. To this day the intangible bonds of guilt tugged at her. They'd been driving to see *her*, and if they hadn't...

Laura closed her eyes. She could still remember how pleased her mother had been when Laura had gotten the scholarships, the student loans and the part-time waitressing job that had enabled her to go to college. "Not that I'm surprised," her mother used to say. "You're going to go far, Laura. It's easier for you than it is for April. You're the smart one in the family."

It hadn't been easier for Laura; it had just looked that way. It still did.

"I didn't mean to upset you," Sam said softly, noting the return of that melancholy look again. "Me and my big mouth..."

"That's okay." As she did whenever someone got too close, she quickly retreated to safer ground. "This pie is really good, isn't it?"

Sam nodded, surprised at how quickly she'd erased the emotion from her face. But when he looked closer, he saw the shadow of sadness that lurked in her brown eyes. That's when he recognized her behavior for what it was, a way of concealing pain. She was hiding. He knew the feeling, he tended to act the same way himself.

"So your family's company really supplied some of the materials for my town house?" she said with a forced cheerfulness. "It's a small world, I guess. I'm really happy with it. The town house, I mean. There's only one thing left for me to do. I'd really like to find a pair of stained glass doors for the front parlor." She was babbling, but to her relief, Sam didn't seem to notice.

"You should come over to the warehouse and take a look around," he suggested. "We've got a number of doors from that period, including some with stained glass or etched glass inlay. We're open on Saturdays. Mitchell and Sons—it's on the edge of town. You can't miss it. I'll even give you a guided tour. What do you say?"

"I don't know..."

"Look at it as my way of repaying you for helping me out tonight."

"You're already paying for my pie and coffee. Besides, I didn't do anything."

"Yes, you did. You made me feel better." He smiled at her. "So how about it? Will you come on Saturday?"

"I'll think about it."

And Laura did think about it, every day for the remainder of the week. She was still brooding about it as she got into her car and headed for work early Saturday morning.

As usual, Hazel was there to greet her. "A little birdie told me that you had a late-night visitor here at the office the other night. I also heard that you and Sam Mitchell were seen eating pie at the B.C. Café that same evening."

"That's right. Sam Mitchell and I were indeed eating pie. Apple pie, Hazel. French apple. And it was very good."

"I don't care what flavor that pie was," Hazel retorted. "Why didn't you tell me about your date?"

"It wasn't a date," Laura denied.

"Then what was it?"

"Hazel, would you please stop badgering poor Dr. Peters," Sandy, the office's dental hygienist, said as she joined them. "You're going to send her running out of here with your questions and we don't want to lose the best children's dentist in town."

"I'm the *only* children's dentist in town," Laura retorted.

"So?" Sandy replied. "That doesn't mean you can't also be the best."

Laura shifted uncomfortably. The art of accepting compliments was one she had yet to master.

"So what's on the agenda today?" Laura asked, eager to redirect the focus away from herself.

"Let's see..." Hazel consulted the appointment book. "We've got Mrs. Boccho bringing in her two-year-old twins for their second visit."

Sandy nodded. "I've got the paints for their clown faces all ready for them."

"Good. Better they get painted than you," Laura stated with a grin. "And who's after the Boccho twins?"

"Doubting Thomas," Hazel said.

Laura nodded. "Ah, the great debate continues on the existence of the tooth fairy. Next?"

"Danette the Yodeler."

"She's not that bad," Laura said. "She's all bark and no bite. I think she has aspirations of being an actress. As soon as she's sitting in the dental chair, she's a real sweetheart."

"They're all real sweethearts once *you've* dealt with them," Sandy pointed out.

"I couldn't do it without you two," Laura replied.

While she was scrubbing up for her first patient, Laura couldn't help wishing that her ability to relate so well with children would rub off on her ability to relate to adults. One adult in particular. Sam Mitchell. She still hadn't decided what to do about his invitation.

It wasn't until Hazel asked her what she planned on doing during her afternoon off that Laura reached a decision. "Oh, I don't know," she said. "I thought I might go check out some stained glass doors for my living room."

Hazel's eyes lighted up with speculation. "Oh, really? Where? At Mitchell and Sons?"

"Possibly."

Hazel gave her a thumbs-up sign. "Good luck."

When Laura arrived at the warehouse, she still wasn't sure she'd made the right decision, but she went inside anyway. She might as well take a look while she was out here, she told herself. Yes, but take a look at the warehouse or take a look at Sam Mitchell? a little voice in her head asked. That was the question.

"She's here!" Sam announced with a pleased grin.

"Who is?" Frank asked.

"It's gotta be the blonde with the great legs," Joey said as he looked out the office window into the warehouse.

"Hey, watch your mouth," Sam cautioned with a glare.

"Since when have you gotten so touchy?" Joey demanded.

"Since he ran into Dr. Peters," Frank answered on Sam's behalf.

"*She* ran into *me*," Sam corrected him.

"You mean *that's* Dr. Peters? The dentist? I don't believe it!"

Sam winced at hearing his own original thoughts repeated out loud by his younger brother. "Why don't you believe it?" he countered. "Just because she's a woman? Lots of women are dentists, you know."

"Hey," Joey exclaimed, "if they all look like that, I'm gonna have to find me a new dentist. Is she taking new patients?"

"She only treats kids," Frank said.

"Too bad," Joey noted.

"Look, you two goons stay here in the office, out of sight, while I go out there and show her around."

"Sure you don't need any help?" Joey asked.

"I'm sure."

But when he saw her again, Sam wasn't so sure; Laura had a way of doing that to him. She also had a way of making him want her so much he couldn't think straight. He wondered what it was about her that made him feel that way. It wasn't just her looks; it was everything about her—the way she moved, the way she talked, even the way she never let him get away with anything.

It hadn't escaped his notice that Laura was wearing a dress—a blue dress. It looked great on her, but it wasn't suitable attire for a trip through the warehouse. It made him wonder if her stop had been a spur-of-the-moment thing. Or was she dressed up because she was going someplace else after this? Unless she'd gotten dressed up for him? He shook his head. Much as he'd like to believe that, he knew she wasn't thinking along those lines. At least, not yet.

* * *

"I see you found us all right."

Laura jumped. She hadn't heard him coming. "Oh, hi." Was that breathless voice really hers? she wondered.

"Hi yourself. You look great."

"I came straight from the office. I look like this all the time. I mean, I didn't dress this way just to come here. That is, I was already wearing this... Anyway, you've got quite a place here. What I mean is... from the little I've seen, it looks very nice." Oh, just give up, she told herself in exasperation.

Sam smiled. "How about that tour I promised you?" he asked.

"That's all right, I'm sure you must be busy." She turned around to leave, convinced coming here had been a big mistake.

But Sam stopped her by putting his hand on her arm. "Wait a minute! Now that you're here, you might as well see the place. Come on. Don't go."

When he said it like that, she found it hard to refuse him, which was all the more reason to say no. This was just another example of Sam's infamous charm. He had the ability to take simple words—like "You look great" or "Don't go"—and fill them with special meaning. He did it with that deep husky voice of his.

Laura sighed. As long as she remembered that he acted this way with every female between the age of nine months and ninety-nine, she'd be fine. Or so she hoped. "Okay. I'll stay for the tour."

"Great. Let's start over here." He led her to a selection of mantelpieces and complete fireplaces.

"I can see why you'd need a lot of room to store these things," Laura noted as they moved on to staircases and banisters.

"You got that right. Storing this stuff—" he indicated an old-fashioned soda fountain counter, complete with stools and an ornate mirror "—was particularly tricky, but I couldn't resist. I found it in a building about to be knocked down and bought it on the spot—the stuff, not the building. It would have been a crime to destroy this." Sam ran an appreciative hand over the solid wood. "It's being shipped to a place in Connecticut next week. It was just what they were looking for, and they were more than willing to pay the price."

"Yo, Sam! Phone call!" someone shouted from the main aisle of the warehouse. "It's MacNamara about the Tandy place."

"Excuse me a minute," Sam said. "This shouldn't take long."

"No problem," she assured him. "Don't hurry. I'll just wait here for you."

Laura waited until Sam had rounded a corner to take an opportunity to resnap a garter that was slowly driving her crazy. Somehow it had come undone, which meant that the front of her stocking was slowly but surely sliding downward. Looking around, she decided that this deserted corner seemed a safe enough place to make a speedy repair.

Taking one final look to make sure no one was in the vicinity, she bent over and quickly gathered the full skirt of her dress—pulling it well above her knee.

She was in the process of refastening the troublesome garter when she heard an approving "Nice. Very nice."

Startled, Laura promptly poked her finger through the delicate nylon stocking she'd been trying to fasten.

"Need any help?" Sam murmured.

"No!" As she straightened, her eyes flew to his. She saw admiration. Appreciation. Hunger. And something else...

Once their eyes met, she couldn't seem to look away. Their surroundings faded into the distance, and time momentarily lost its importance as everything—breathing, thinking—was put on hold. Everything except feeling. And she was doing plenty of that as an unspoken recognition flowed between them.

Reality eventually returned, and as it did so, Laura belatedly realized that the hem of her dress was still slightly askew. Looking away from Sam, she nervously smoothed the jersey material back into place.

"I didn't hear you coming back," she said, because it was the first coherent thing that came to a mind recently gone blank.

"The call didn't take as long as I thought it would."

It hadn't taken as long as Laura thought it would, either, but she decided not to dwell on that. Better to pretend that nothing had happened. Which shouldn't be too difficult, she told herself. After all, pretending was something she'd been doing for quite a long time.

But as Sam continued with the rest of his tour, Laura found it hard to focus her scattered attention on what he was saying. Instead she was noticing little things about him, like the way he walked. It was a cowboy kind of walk, but she couldn't figure out why she had that impression. The swing of his hips, maybe? Or was it the masculine cockiness of his steps?

And she couldn't help but notice the way his broad shoulders tapered to a lean waist and narrow hips. After all, he *was* walking in front of her as they passed through a doorway leading from one section of the warehouse to another.

Distracted as she was by Sam's body, she ended up tripping over the raised threshold. She would have gone flying had Sam not turned around in time to catch her—in his arms.

"Careful," he murmured softly.

Good advice, she thought with hazy logic. But it was too late. She was already held so close to him that the idea of being careful seemed to melt away.

Once again their eyes met and caught.

"Are you okay?" he asked huskily.

She didn't have a clue. All she knew was that she could actually feel the minty freshness of his breath gently caressing her lips as he spoke.

Her eyes lowered to his mouth, which hovered mere inches from hers. He was giving her time to refuse. She knew that, but she simply couldn't muster the willpower to say no. She didn't *want* to refuse; she wanted him to kiss her.

And he did. Softly at first. It was just the sheerest hint of a kiss, and it felt so good that Laura had to close her eyes. He slid his hands around her back as he smoothly moved her closer into his embracing arms. And all the while he was gently brushing his lips across hers—back and forth—until Laura thought she'd go crazy for wanting more.

He soon gave her more, deepening the kiss as he felt her response to him grow. It was a slow build-up, a shared escalation from tantalizing nibbles to parted lips. From there things began progressing rapidly, as any earlier tentativeness evaporated in a fire of passion.

Laura had just slid her arms around Sam's neck when the sound of a blaring horn made her jump. She broke away from him like a guilty teenager caught necking, which was exactly how she felt. Embarrassed yet exhilarated.

"Sorry, boss," the forklift driver who'd sounded his horn was saying to Sam. "I didn't realize it was you."

"Just don't do it again," Sam said in a distracted voice. He may have been speaking to his employee, but he couldn't take his eyes off Laura.

"It's getting late. I really should be going," she said softly. And I really should try to get myself together again, she warned herself, but she found it impossible to listen to her conscience.

"Wait..." But just as Sam took her hand in his, they were interrupted again.

"Sam, phone call!" someone bellowed from another part of the warehouse. "They need you in the office, pronto!"

Muttering under his breath, he reluctantly let her go. "We're obviously not going to get any privacy here. But later... I'll call you when I'm through here tonight," he promised her.

She nodded and left. As she walked away, it didn't feel as if her feet touched the ground once.

Sam couldn't keep his thoughts off Laura and the kiss they'd shared. His unusual preoccupation was eventually noticed by his two brothers, not to mention their trusty secretary.

"What's wrong with you this afternoon?" Mabel demanded when, for the third time, Sam gave her back a stack of work sheets minus his requested signature. "You got spring fever or something?"

"Is that any way to talk to your boss?" Sam returned somewhat absently.

"It is when my boss forgets how to sign his own name."

Sam frowned at her. It was meant to intimidate Mabel, but deep down he knew it wouldn't work.

And he was right; she didn't budge an inch. She merely kept glaring at him.

At this point, Joey ambled into the office.

"It's not spring," he stated, putting in his two cents. "It's that dentist."

"What dentist?" Mabel demanded, clearly upset that something was going on that she didn't know about.

"The one Sam's chasing," Joey replied.

"Since when has Sam had to chase women?" Mabel countered. "They usually chase him."

"Get out of here, Mabel," Sam said in exasperation. "Go do some work. And just for the record—women do not chase me. Pursue maybe, but not chase."

"So tell me about this dentist," Mabel ordered Joey, ignoring Sam's orders to leave.

"Her name's Laura Peters," Joey replied, "and she's a children's dentist. She's got great legs, but Sam didn't appreciate me noticing that fact."

"I don't think your wife would appreciate it, either," Mabel retorted sharply. "Stick to the facts."

Joey grinned. "You'll have to ask Sam about those, although one of the guys said he caught big brother here and the dentist in a hot clinch."

Sam's expression hardened. "That's enough."

Sam rarely used that tone of voice, but when he did, Mabel knew he was no longer kidding. She muttered something about having work to finish and left.

Joey tried to make a similarly hasty retreat, but Sam stopped him.

"Listen, little brother, I already told you to watch your mouth. Now I'll tell you this once and then I don't want to have to repeat myself. I don't want you talking about Laura. Plain and simple. You got that?"

"Hey, what's the big deal here? You're not really serious about her, are you?" Joey asked.

"That's no business of yours."

Joey looked confused. In a small way, Sam could empathize with that. He was feeling pretty confused himself right now.

"For God's sake, Sam. She's a dentist!"

"What's that got to do with anything?" he retorted.

"Aside from the fact that you hate dentists, it's got a hell of a lot to do with it. The woman is a doctor. We're talking major bucks here. Beautiful clothes, fancy car. Did you know that she drives a BMW? I went outside to check it out. That car alone cost more than my entire house. We're talking another world here. She's not exactly 'plain folks.' You know what I mean?''

"So she makes a lot of money."

"A lot more than you do."

Sam shifted uncomfortably.

"I'll bet her office doesn't look anything like this one does," Joey said.

Sam looked around. Now that Joey mentioned it... How long had those crooked venetian blinds hung in that window? They had to be even older than Mabel. And they bore no resemblance to the bright, trendy miniblinds Laura had in her waiting room. As for all those leafy plants she had artistically placed throughout her office, the only greenery here came from the faded dollar bill hanging on the wall. And what importance did his bowling trophies have when stacked against the string of degrees on her wall? Not much.

"We need to redecorate this place," Sam growled.

"What's the point?" Joey retorted. "You're never going to get it to look as good as hers does."

"It doesn't have to look this bad."

"You never minded the way it looked before," Joey pointed out.

"I wasn't paying attention."

"And you are paying attention now, right? Attention to the lady dentist. Look, all I'm saying is that a woman like Dr. Peters is obviously used to the best things in life. One look at her will tell you that. We're talking major class here. I mean ritzy. *Real* ritzy. I mean well-off. *Real* well-off. And I mean educated. *Real*—''

"I know what you mean," Sam said irritably.

"Hey, don't get me wrong. Chasing her is fine. Just don't catch her."

Sam took exception to getting advice from Joey. "Do I look like I'm stupid?"

"You already thought of all this yourself?"

Actually Sam hadn't, but he wasn't about to admit that fact.

Joey took his silence to mean yes. "Well, that's a relief. But when you got so touchy about her, I thought . . . Never mind what I thought."

Sam didn't know what to think, but he had to admit that Joey did have a point. When you got right down to it, he and Laura didn't have much in common—aside from that incredible kiss they'd shared. And though he certainly valued that moment, it didn't change the cold, hard facts. What could he, a working-class guy who'd never even attended college, have in common with a classy lady dentist? Not much.

"You really had me going there for a while," Joey was saying. "I should have remembered what a practical joker you are. Always the kidder, huh, Sam?"

Sam had the sinking feeling that this time the joke was on him.

Four

Laura felt like dancing. Right there in the middle of her living room she felt like kicking off her shoes and dancing. So she did. She even started singing along with the classic-rock radio station playing on her stereo.

It didn't matter that her voice wasn't made for singing or her feet for dancing. The wonderfully euphoric feeling she'd had since Sam had kissed her was still humming through her, making her feel as if she could do anything. But just to keep things from getting too out of hand, she grabbed a watering can and began watering her plants in between dance steps.

"And here's another golden oldie, folks," the radio announcer said as one song faded into the next. "See if you can remember this Dave Clark Five hit from the sixties."

"Glad All Over" suddenly blasted from the speakers. And Laura not only felt glad all over, she also felt excited, nervous . . . and more than a little out of breath.

"You're getting out of shape," she scolded herself as she boogied from a philodendron plant to a Boston fern. "It's either that or it's Sam...." Her voice trailed off, and her eyes became dreamy as she recalled the feel of his lips on hers. The next thing she knew, water was running over the edge of the planter and down onto her bare feet.

When the phone rang an instant later, Laura lunged for it, the dripping water completely forgotten. "Hello?"

"Please don't hang up just because this is a recording," a metallic computer-generated voice intoned. "If you'd like to hear about our lifetime aluminum siding guarantee, please press one..."

Laura didn't press one. She hung up, more than a little irritated. Aside from hating computerized sales calls, she was doubly resentful because the caller hadn't been Sam. She checked her watch. It was after five already. The warehouse was closed now. Surely he'd be getting in touch with her soon.

She didn't know exactly what she was going to say to Sam when he did call. She didn't want to think that far ahead yet. She didn't want this magical feeling to lessen by thinking about it too much. For the moment it was enough to simply enjoy it, to take a break from her customary round of doubts and uncertainty.

But that break from uncertainty didn't last long once Sam was on the line. She noticed right away how uncharacteristically distant and formal he sounded.

"I'm sorry I wasn't able to continue your tour this afternoon," he said. "I never did get around to showing you those etched glass doors you wanted to see."

"That's okay." She didn't know what else to say. This wasn't the way she'd expected their conversation to begin. It was so impersonal, so businesslike. So very unlike Sam.

"If you'd give me the dimensions of the threshold, perhaps I could narrow down the selection process for you," he suggested in a friendly yet brisk voice.

"All right."

"Fine."

Silence. Laura knew Sam was still on the line; she could hear him breathing. But he wasn't saying anything. So she did. "I meant to ask you, how is your baby nephew doing?"

"Fine. He'll be out of the incubator tomorrow. Frank and Anne named him Frank Jr. Real original, I know," he noted dryly. Sam couldn't imagine Laura calling any son of hers Junior anything. No, her son would have some classy-sounding name—Randall or Nelson. And he'd own his own BMW by the time he was sixteen. Sam sighed.

Laura heard him. "Is something wrong?" she asked.

"What could be wrong?" he countered.

"I don't know. Are you still worried about the baby's...I mean about Frank Jr.'s health?"

"No, I'm not worried about anything." He'd gone beyond being worried several hours ago. Now he was just plain depressed.

"Oh. I thought you sounded a little...I don't know...a little unlike yourself," Laura concluded weakly.

"I've been sounding unlike myself a lot lately. Must be something going around. You don't sound quite like yourself, either," he pointed out, not wanting to be the only one who was squirming here.

"Maybe we have a bad connection."

"Yeah, maybe we do." It was still a connection that was too damn powerful for his peace of mind, Sam noted. Hearing her voice brought her vividly to mind. It also brought their kiss to mind—the softness of her lips, the warmth of her response...

He shifted in his office chair, very much aware of the tricks his body was playing on him. Hell, he wasn't a teenager anymore. But then Laura was no girl, she was a woman... She was a lady, he corrected himself. A rich lady dentist who had no right affecting him this way, he concluded with an aggrieved shake of his head.

"Sam, are you still there?" she asked.

"Oh, I'm here, all right." Very much so. *Too* much so. "Listen, about those glass doors..."

Laura listened as Sam went on at some length explaining how she should take the measurements.

"Was there anything else?" she asked him, wanting to give him every possible chance to bring up that kiss.

"No, that about takes care of everything."

"Fine," she said coolly.

"Great."

There didn't seem to be much else left to say. "Goodbye, then."

"Laura..."

"Yes?" she said, trying not to sound too hopeful.

There was another one of those heavy silences, the kind that was tying her stomach in knots. And then he said, "Remember to call me with those dimensions."

"I won't forget." But apparently he had. Forgotten all about... Hearing the dial tone, she hung up the phone.

Any desire she'd had to sing or dance had long since evaporated. Other desires weren't as easily erased, however. Like the desire to know what the hell was going on. Or the desire to knock some sense into one Sam Mitchell. What was his problem? Why had he kissed her as if there was no tomorrow, and then acted as if it had never happened? Surely he couldn't have overlooked the way she'd responded to him?

From the way he was acting, she could only conclude that the kiss hadn't meant anything to him. Or at the very least, it had meant much more to *her* than it had to *him*.

She abruptly switched off the radio, annoyed by the up-beat song. Her previously joyous mood had nose-dived right into the basement. So she headed straight for the kitchen and her cache of frozen goodies.

It wasn't until she was on her second bowl of Cherry Garcia ice cream, her own personal prescription for a bad case of the blues, that it suddenly hit her. The look on Sam's face after he'd kissed her hadn't been one of amusement or indifference. It had been one of wonder and astonishment.

Now that she thought about it, he'd looked as downright shell-shocked as she'd felt. Which meant that he hadn't been as unaffected as he'd later pretended to be during their phone call. Maybe he'd gotten cold feet?

She took another bite of ice cream and nodded to herself. The more she thought about it, the more likely that possibility became. She certainly preferred it to the other explanations she'd come up with. And, heaven knew, it was definitely a reaction she could empathize with.

Actually she wasn't sure why she hadn't gotten a similar case of the jitters herself. Normally she was overly cautious. Other people thought twice; she thought three or four times. She'd never been the type to jump into anything. But there had been something incredibly special about their kiss.

She sighed and stuck her spoon into the ice cream carton, eating it directly from there now that her bowl was empty. Her willpower was nil where this dessert was concerned. She worried that the same thing might be true about her willpower with Sam. What if he was as addictive as Cherry Garcia ice cream? What if one bite wasn't enough? What if she wanted the whole carton?

"One step at a time," she told herself.

There was nothing she could do about the situation now, anyway. She wasn't about to call Sam and ask him if he had cold feet. He'd think she was nuts. And what if that wasn't his reason for being distant? No, she'd play it by ear—give him a few days and see what happened. Meanwhile she'd measure the doorway for those doors and at least keep that particular line of communication open.

Their next three phone calls were as baffling to Laura as the first one had been. As far as lines of communication went, the calls were okay, but they fell far short of her expectations and hopes. Oh, sure, Sam was friendly, but it was in a casual sort of way, different from the way he'd treated her before.

The bottom line was that he simply wasn't pursuing her the way he had been. The flirtatious banter she'd come to expect from him was gone. And she missed it, almost as much as she missed seeing him.

Exactly one week had passed when Laura decided she couldn't stand the suspense any longer. One way or another she had to know where she stood. And the only way to do that was to come face-to-face with Sam, something she hadn't done since he'd kissed her. She was sure that once she looked in his eyes, she'd know if he was trying to let her down gently. Besides, she had a good reason for going to the warehouse. It was time to pick out the doors.

This time Laura was the one to catch Sam off guard. He was talking to one of the workers when she walked up behind him.

He gave the phrase "sight for sore eyes" new meaning. Just looking at him made her feel good. Full of butterflies, to be sure, but also filled with an indescribable feeling, as if an empty space had just been filled.

So she stood there a moment, running her eyes over him as discreetly as possible while not missing one single detail. His dark hair curled over the back of his shirt collar. He had a measuring tape haphazardly sticking out of the back pocket of his jeans. As he signed something on a clipboard, she realized that he was left-handed.

She savored the moment of discovery. This was something she'd learned about him herself, something Hazel had omitted telling her.

"Hi, there," she said softly.

He turned, and she knew. Just from the way he was looking at her, she knew. Whatever was between them was felt as powerfully by him as it was by her.

"Hi, yourself," he said as softly. "No dress this time, I see."

She smiled. "You remembered."

"Yeah." I remembered, all right, Sam thought to himself. Not only the dress. Everything. Right down to the smallest detail of that white lacy garter she'd been fixing. "So, how are you doing?"

"Fine. Busy."

"Yeah. Me, too," he agreed.

"Um..." Without Laura's even being aware of it, her fidgety fingers headed straight for the pockets in her cotton cardigan. "I thought jeans might be more appropriate attire for picking out a door. What do you think?"

That you look too damn good in them. "Jeans are fine. I wear them quite a bit myself."

"I noticed."

"Yeah, well, maybe I should show you those doors I promised you."

What about the rest of what you promised? Laura silently wondered. What about that kiss?

Had she been a confrontational person, she would have asked those questions and demanded answers. But that wasn't her style. There were, however, other ways of getting answers. First she had to get him to come to dinner at her place so they could talk without distractions. No, she corrected herself ruefully. *First* she had to get up the nerve to invite him.

"These are the doors I told you about," Sam said as he leaned the first one up against a sawhorse for her inspection. "The stained glass work is particularly good, don't you think?" Right, Sam thought to himself in disgust. You sound like a damn museum curator.

"They're lovely. I'll take them."

"But you haven't seen the others yet," he said.

Laura knew it didn't matter; these were the ones she wanted. She'd been shopping around long enough to know the right thing when she saw it. But looking at others would give her additional time with Sam—time to build up the nerve to ask him to dinner. "Okay, show me the others."

As he did so, she continued racking her brain to come up with some clever way to casually slip an invitation into the conversation. *You know, it's funny you should mention antique hinges because they've certainly always fascinated me, so why not come over to my place for dinner and we'll discuss the subject further?*

No, too late, she thought to herself. He was already off the subject of hinges and on to the advantages of oak versus pine. Okay, then, *I've always been fascinated by wood....*

"Would you like to come to dinner?" she ended up blurting.

"What?"

His startled reaction was not very encouraging. "Dinner," she said succinctly. "At my place. Tomorrow night." Not the smoothest of invitations, she admitted to herself, but she'd had to get the words out before she lost her nerve. After all, she was on unfamiliar ground here. All of this was quite new to her.

While normally she went out of her way to make sure her inner nervousness didn't show, today she didn't seem to be having much success at playing the role of a composed dentist. To her ears she sounded as awkward as she had when called upon to read aloud in grade school. Her voice had trembled and cracked then, too.

"You're inviting me to dinner?" Sam repeated, as if wanting to make sure he got this right. When she nodded, he said, "Why?"

"To eat," she retorted. "Look, if you don't want to come—"

"I didn't say that."

Then say something, she wanted to shout, but figured she'd made enough of a fool of herself for one day as it was. So she remained silent.

"What time?" he asked.

"Six."

"Fine, I'll be there."

"You will?"

Sam nodded.

"Okay," she said.

"Okay," he repeated.

He looked at her, she looked at him, and they both smiled—sharing a moment that shouldn't have been special but was. It was as if when they forgot to think, they were able to communicate better. There was a visual link. A bond.

The invisible ties were broken when Sam gritted his teeth and looked away. Determined not to lose more ground than he had already, he briskly returned to the matter at hand. "Now what about these doors . . . ?"

"Dinner, huh?" Hazel was saying, her speculation clearly audible to Laura over the phone lines. "Your place? Just you and Sam?"

"Hazel, I thought you called to ask me about the missing Wajinski file."

"Nah, that was just an excuse. I *really* called to find out how it went at Sam's warehouse. I knew you were going over there this afternoon. But I didn't know you were going to ask him to dinner.''

Laura was already regretting letting it slip that Sam was coming over tomorrow night. But she'd had to talk to someone, and Hazel happened to have called at the right moment. "It's not any big deal or anything. I mean, it's only dinner.''

"To start off with. Who knows where it could go from there. Listen, want a few tips from a pro?"

While Laura was trying to come up with a polite way of saying no, Hazel went right on. "Trust me. I know what I'm talking about here. Wear your best perfume, light some candles—''

"And pray, right?" Laura inserted wryly.

"Hey, you almost sound nervous."

"Maybe that's because I *am* nervous. I feel...I don't know. Like I'm chasing after him or something.''

Laura didn't know whether to be insulted or relieved when Hazel laughed. "Don't be ridiculous. Sam's had women chasing after him before, and they didn't act this way at all.''

"Gee, thanks," Laura retorted. "Somehow that doesn't make me feel better.''

"I wonder why that is. After all, you did say this was just a simple dinner, right?''

"Right. Just a simple dinner. Well, thanks for calling, Hazel. I'll see you in the office Monday morning.''

"You mean I have to wait until then for the details?" Hazel demanded.

"There won't be any details, so don't hold your breath," Laura warned her.

"Spoilsport.''

Laura didn't have time to worry about Hazel's grumbling. She was too busy spending the rest of the night worrying about everything else; from what to serve for dinner, to what she'd wear, to the cobwebs she'd noticed in the corner of her living room ceiling.

By four o'clock the next afternoon her town house was spotless, the dinner menu was complete, but she still hadn't decided what to wear. If Sam came wearing jeans tonight, and there was no reason to suppose he wouldn't, she didn't want to appear overdressed for the occasion. Laura wanted everything to be just right. That meant the house in perfect order, the food cooked to perfection and herself looking as good as possible given the fact that she'd slept only five hours last night.

With that thought in mind, she finally settled on a tropical-print skirt and a matching turquoise jewel-necked top. The skirt's bright colors had always made her feel rather bold in the past, and she was hoping the outfit would do the same for her tonight. Besides, the skirt had pockets, and she had a feeling her trembling fingers might need a safe refuge tonight.

Sam rang her doorbell at precisely six o'clock. A quick look in the hall mirror assured her that she looked... nervous.

She took a deep breath and opened the front door—to find Sam examining her door's hinges.

"Nice hardware," he said admiringly. "Here, I got these for you." He held up two bottles of wine. "Didn't know which one would be right for tonight."

"Thank you."

"Hope they're okay."

"They're fine," she said.

Sam heaved a silent sigh of relief. Old Smitty down at the Lucky Liquor Store had told him he couldn't go wrong with that choice. But since he knew that Smitty, like himself, preferred beer to wine, he hadn't been sure it was safe to trust the recommendation. But then Sam wasn't sure it was

safe to have accepted Laura's invitation in the first place.
Yet here he was anyway.

"Come on in," Laura invited him. "I'll go put these
bottles in to chill." While she was at it, she wondered if she
shouldn't put herself in to chill, as well. She felt incredibly
hot and bothered. Sam made her feel that way. And she had
guessed right; he was indeed wearing jeans and a crisp white
shirt, although he'd dressed them up somewhat by adding
a honey-brown corduroy jacket and a navy blue tie. "Sit
down and make yourself comfortable."

Noticing the way he was eyeing the French provincial lines
of her couch—as if the thing were a delicate absurdity in-
capable of supporting a feather—she felt compelled to give
him some reassurance. "It's okay. You can sit on it. It's
sturdier than it looks."

He shouldn't have come, Sam told himself as he gingerly
sat down. He was only asking for trouble. But he hadn't
been able to resist her invitation. She'd looked at him with
those big brown eyes of hers, and he'd been lost.

"Would you like some wine now, or later with dinner?"
she asked.

Sam really wanted a beer. "Later would be fine."

"Okay. I'll be right back." She returned from the kitchen
within a few seconds. Cranking up her nerve, she took a seat
next to him on the sofa. "So, tell me," she said brightly,
"how's Frank Jr. doing?"

"Fine. He'll be out of the hospital next week. Meanwhile
my parents are back from Florida and they've practically
camped out in the maternity ward. Frank Jr. is their first
grand*son* and my dad's really going overboard."

"You're lucky to have such a supportive family," she said
somewhat wistfully.

"Having a supportive family is like anything else," he
replied. "It's got its good and its bad points."

Laura could identify with that. At the moment, sitting next to Sam on the couch had its good and its bad points, too. Laura was closer to him, yet still farther away than she wanted to be. How to make a move? She should at least wait until after dinner, shouldn't she?

"Would you like an hors d'oeuvre?" she asked him. Without waiting for him to answer, she held up a tray for his perusal. She also leaned a tad closer to him. She wished she had the courage to say, "crackers, celery sticks or me?" She had no idea flirting was this hard.

Sam stared at the silver tray filled with a variety of delicate little somethings. Was he supposed to pick them up with his fingers? No chips and dip here. No sirree, this stuff was ... he didn't have a clue. "What is this?"

"Stuffed mushroom caps."

"Oh. Right." He took one; it seemed rude not to after asking about it. He was relieved to see that she took one, too, and used her fingers the same way he had.

"They're a bit messy to eat, I'm afraid," she said after dabbing at her lips with a napkin.

As silence descended once again, she struggled for something inviting to say. All she could come up with was "I'm glad you were able to come over this evening."

"Yeah, well ..."

To her disappointment, Sam shifted in his seat, moving away from her, supposedly to reach for a celery stick. Her self-confidence took another dip when they proceeded to the dinner table a few minutes later.

"You didn't have to go to all this trouble for me," Sam said, staring in disbelief at the incredibly formal-looking table. "Paper plates would've been fine."

"It was no trouble," she fibbed.

"What are the candles for?" he asked.

The better to seduce you with, my dear? The words came
to her mind but not to her lips. "The candles? Oh, they're
for an added touch of elegant dining."

"That means I shouldn't tuck my dinner napkin under my
chin, right?" he inquired mockingly.

"I don't know what it means," she muttered, feeling
awkward and self-conscious. Damn, the candles *were* too
obvious.

"Aren't you going to light them?"

"No. They're just for decoration." Laura whisked the
offending candlesticks off the table and onto a sideboard.
She then took the lid off the porcelain soup tureen and
dipped in a ladle. "If you'll hand me your bowl, I'll serve
the soup."

When she returned the bowl to him, Sam looked at it as
if it might bite.

"It's borscht," she said. "You know, beet soup."

"Oh."

First the mushroom caps, now this. She was really bat-
ting a thousand here, Laura thought. "I can get you something else if you'd prefer."

"No, this is fine. I've never had beet soup before. What's
the white stuff on top?"

"Sour cream," she replied.

"Oh."

Noting the cautious way he lifted the soup spoon to his
mouth, Laura decided she should have stuck to something
basic; something tried-and-true, as she'd done for the rest
of the meal. Besides, borscht wasn't exactly romantic unless you were one-quarter Ukrainian, the way she was.

"Hey, this isn't half-bad," Sam murmured.

"Thanks." The words of praise, slight though they may
have been, bolstered her sagging spirits. "It's an old family
recipe. Originally from my Ukrainian grandmother, up-
dated by my cousin."

"The one with the restaurant?"

Laura nodded. "April is the one who came up with the idea of using a blender. Just pour in beef bouillon and beets, then add a touch of lemon juice. That's all it takes."

"It tastes good." He took another spoonful. "So your grandmother was Ukrainian?"

Laura nodded. "You sound surprised."

He was. Did classy blue bloods usually have Ukrainian grandmothers? He didn't know. Unless her grandmother had been a Ukrainian countess or something. Yeah, that fit.

Laura wondered about the strange look that passed over Sam's face. Was it the fault of the borscht? Or was it due to the smell of burning steaks coming from the kitchen?

"Excuse me a minute!" Her hasty departure from the dinner table prevented the meat from becoming too charbroiled, but it had passed the medium-rare stage she'd been aiming for.

"Everything all right in there?" Sam asked from the dining room.

"Fine," she called back, infinitely grateful for the swinging café doors that shielded most of the kitchen from view. They should have gone out to a restaurant, she decided. She'd forgotten what a big deal cooking at home was; forgotten how much time and energy it took. Time and energy that should have been expended on talking to Sam. After all, that was the whole reason for this get-together. To find out how Sam felt. What he thought.

She could well imagine what he was thinking at the moment—that she was a real flake who served beet soup and burned steaks. A woman who put out candles to intimidate rather than to seduce. The evening was not proceeding the way she'd planned, or hoped.

"It's not over yet," she reminded herself. "Don't give up so easily."

"Did you say something?" Sam asked.

"I'll be right there," she replied.

Despite her brief pep talk to herself, the more scintillating and seductive she tried to be, the stupider she felt. Sam didn't seem to be catching any of the hints she was dropping. He did notice the way she kept looking at his hands, however, and he didn't seem real pleased by it.

"What's wrong?" he demanded. "Am I holding my fork wrong or something?"

"No. It's just that you're left-handed." She was about to go on to say that she had a soft spot for lefties when Sam interrupted her.

"Yeah, I'm left-handed. Something wrong with that?"

"Nothing at all," she hastily assured him. "A lot of people are left-handed. My cousin, for one. She's also the cook in the family," she noted with a rueful look at their steak. "I'm afraid the meat was a little overdone."

"I like mine well-done," Sam stated. "And your cousin may be the cook in the family, but I'll bet you're the brains."

Talk like that made Laura feel uncomfortable. "I wouldn't say that."

"Why not? Why are you so defensive about being smart?"

"I'm not defensive. And if I'm so smart, you'd think I'd be able to cook a simple steak without burning it."

"Anyone can cook a steak."

"You'd think so, wouldn't you? But apparently that's not the case. Are you ready for dessert? It'll be better than this, I promise."

Sam caught hold of her hand as she was about to sail past him.

"I liked the meal," he said quietly. "I liked everything."

"Even the borscht?"

"Even the borscht."

She smiled. "I'm glad."

After their Kahlúa parfait, which was as good as she'd claimed it would be, they retired to the living room for coffee. She decided to sit next to him on the couch again, only a little closer this time.

"Would you care for an after-dinner drink?" she asked.

"No, thanks."

Silence. She supposed that was as good a place to begin as any other. "You've been rather quiet this evening," she noted. "Is everything all right?"

"Fine."

No luck there so she tried a different tack. "I'll bet you're wondering why I invited you over for dinner tonight."

"Not really," he said.

"Oh."

"Why? Was there something you wanted to tell me?"

She shook her head, then shrugged. "I just wanted to thank you for all the help you've given me selecting the new doors."

"No problem."

After an uncomfortable silence, she forced herself to go on. "There was one other thing...."

"Yes?"

"You know I've said before that you seemed quiet, or unlike yourself, the past week or so. Not that I really know you well enough to know what constitutes 'unlike yourself,'" she hurriedly added. "I mean, maybe you do act like this normally."

"Act like what?"

You're not flirting with me anymore. I'm trying to give you the green light here, and you're not paying attention to the traffic! But she couldn't say that. "Um, you don't seem as...as outgoing as you usually are. I just wondered... I mean..." She took a deep breath and tried again. "Is it my fault? Have I said or done anything to make you feel ill at ease?"

"You're the one who seems ill at ease," Sam pointed out.

"You're absolutely right. It's just that . . . I'm no good at this!" she muttered.

"Good at what?"

"Seducing men."

Sam almost choked on his coffee. "Wha-*what*?"

"You heard me the first time. I certainly don't intend to repeat it a second time," she said, annoyed by his obtuseness.

Leaning forward, Sam carefully set the delicate coffee cup onto its matching saucer. "I'm obviously missing something here. Care to explain it to me?"

She shook her head. "Forget it. Chalk it up to a full moon or something. I realize I'm not making any sense to you. I misunderstood... I made a mistake. I just didn't want any awkwardness to remain as a result of that episode at the warehouse last week."

"Episode?" he repeated.

"That kiss, damn it!" she said in an aggravated tone of voice. "It was no big deal. I know that. But you've been acting strangely ever since."

"If it was no big deal, why are you asking me about it now?"

"Never mind. This was a bad idea to begin with. You've already got half the town chasing after you, you certainly don't need any hassle from me."

"You got that right. I don't need any hassle from you."

Her heart sank even lower.

"What I need is this . . ." He took her into his arms and kissed her.

Five

Being kissed by Sam was even better than Laura remembered. So was kissing him back. It was like Christmas and the Fourth of July all rolled up in one. Fireworks. Excitement. Bright colored lights. Joy.

Laura trembled beneath the force of her emotions. She couldn't believe he was actually kissing her with such unabashed passion; couldn't believe the depth of his hunger. But Sam soon made a believer out of her.

This was no teasing dalliance. This was rough and soft, searing and intense. This was Sam—and he was kissing her as if intent on proving his feelings for her.

He wanted her. He told her so with every stroke of his tongue, every touch of his hand. He wanted her closer, nearer, responding to him as he was responding to her. He got what he wanted. Laura melted into his embrace; leaning against him, wrapping her arms around his waist and hanging on as the world whirled around her.

Passion prevailed as she became an equal participant in the seductive magic, giving as much pleasure as she was receiving. She explored him as he was exploring her, with caressing lips and seductive hands. She did some of the things she'd longed to do, dreamed of doing. She ran her fingers through the long, thick, curly hair at the back of his neck. She compared the taste of his full lower lip to his curvy upper lip and found both to her liking. He was as addictive as Cherry Garcia ice cream, she thought to herself with hazy wonder. Even better than Kahlúa parfait.

Her explorations were momentarily put on hold as Sam slid his hands beneath her top. The first time his fingers brushed her bare back she felt the electricity clear down to her toes. Her gasp was quickly followed by a husky murmur of pleasure as he lowered her to the couch.

Their semihorizontal position afforded new pleasures to be savored. The weight of his body on hers and the unmistakable feel of his arousal filled her with a new kind of hunger. She lay there breathless with anticipation as his hands moved from her back, around her waist, climbing her ribs one by one until his widespread fingers were poised at the base of her breast.

And then, suddenly, it was over as abruptly as it had begun. Sam wrenched himself away, leaving Laura lying there feeling dazed and deserted. Humiliation rushed over her like a tidal wave, staining her face red with color and her heart gray with shame.

She'd laid it all out for him, responded like a wanton woman and made a complete fool of herself. Now she had to gather the tattered remnants of her dignity long enough for him to leave. Then she could cry. Then and only then.

For now she needed to put some space between herself and the man who'd given her such pleasure only to cause her such pain. It took all the strength she possessed not to scramble to her feet and run from the room. Instead she sat up, sliding as far away from him as possible. She then rose from the couch with what she thought was remarkable grace, given the fact that her knees were shaking so badly she wasn't even sure they'd hold her up.

Sam silently cursed himself as he saw her physically and emotionally withdrawing from him. For once he could read her thoughts clearly. She was hurting as badly as he was.

Before she could move even farther away, he reached out for her arm, halting her retreat. "Look, don't misunderstand me..."

She immediately pulled her arm away. "Oh, I think I understand very well," she said in an artificially calm voice. "You've made it pretty clear. No need to explain. I may be a bit dense, but I'm not stupid."

"Of course you're not stupid. You've got a million degrees on your wall proving how smart you are!"

"They don't prove anything," she said flatly.

"They prove how different we are, you and me."

"Fine. We're very different. I'm sorry I embarrassed you by inviting you over here tonight."

"You didn't embarrass me."

"Just myself apparently. Would you like some more coffee before you leave?" she asked pointedly.

"No, I'd like to..." He broke off. Most of the things he'd like to do involved taking her to bed and doing things to her that were still illegal in some states.

"It really is getting late," she said in the same politely conversational tone.

"You can drop the pleasant-hostess routine," he growled. "I'm trying to tell you that I didn't stop kissing you because I wanted to stop. I stopped because..." Pausing, he ran a distracted hand through his hair as he searched for the right words to say. "You drive a BMW, for God's sake," he finally bit out.

"So?" she retorted defensively. "Is there something wrong with that?"

"You're way out of my league, lady!" The words were spoken with grim impatience.

"Is that what you think? Is that what this is all about?"

"Yes."

"I'm really not that different," Laura murmured huskily. "I'm not what you think I am. If you only knew..."

"Knew what?"

She shook her head, unable to continue.

"Anyway," he went on, "I got to thinking—an incredibly successful lady dentist and a working-class guy like me? Not exactly a match made in heaven. You deserve better," he said gruffly.

"Maybe you're the one who deserves better," she whispered unsteadily. She had to wait until her emotions were once again under control before being able to continue. "I'm not *incredibly* successful. But even if I was, you've got nothing to be ashamed of."

"I didn't say I was ashamed. Just outclassed. Hell, I wasn't even sure I was using the right spoon with my soup."

"I wasn't born knowing which spoon to use, you know."

"I'll bet you were. It's instinctive with you. As much a part of you as your blond hair and your great legs."

"Not really," she retorted dryly. "Trust me. It wasn't until I was in high school that I even knew there was such a thing as a soup spoon. As for the class you say I've got, I've acquired that along the way. And if I can do it, anyone can."

He shook his head. "Not me."

"That's what I used to say."

"Meaning what? That you're offering to take me in hand and give me culture lessons?"

"Maybe I'm offering to take you in hand, period."

Her words created a moment of electric silence.

"I can't believe I said that," she muttered, looking away from him.

"Neither can I." He grinned. "But I definitely liked the sound of it. I was just about to suggest the same thing myself."

"I'm usually not like this. I mean, I don't make a practice out of..."

"Inviting men to dinner and then trying to seduce them?" He gently touched her flushed cheek. "That's good news."

"You're doing it again," she said.

"Doing what?"

"Making me smile when I least expect it. I've been a nervous wreck all evening, you know."

He looked surprised. "Really? You could have fooled me."

"You didn't pick up on any of the hints I was giving you."

"What hints?"

"I sat down next to you on the couch," she said, as if that were a major accomplishment.

"Yeah. So?"

"So you didn't do anything."

"I didn't think you'd appreciate it if I jumped you while you were offering me fancy appetizers," he noted ruefully.

"I'm not very good at expressing myself, I guess." So far as she was concerned, there was no guessing about it. She'd never been able to get her feelings across very well. "It's easy for you," she told him. "You're outgoing. You get on well with everyone."

"And you don't?" he retorted.

She shrugged. "I'm a dentist. People aren't usually drawn to dentists. You said so yourself. And I'm not at all outgoing."

"You're not exactly shy, either."

Oh, but I am, she longed to tell him, but knew what his reaction would be. One of disbelief. *Shy? You? No way.* She'd heard it before. So she kept quiet.

"What are you trying to say?" Sam demanded. "That you're not the self-confident superwoman you appear to be?"

She looked at him in dismay. "Is that how you see me?"

"I see you as one very sexy lady. One I haven't quite figured out yet, but I'm working on it."

"I'm not sexy." When he was about to protest, she held up her hand. "No, really. I'm not just saying that so you'll tell me I *am* sexy."

"Why don't you think you're sexy?"

What could she say? That her hips were too heavy, her tummy not flat enough, her bra size too small? She didn't want him knowing that about her yet. Her fear—one of them, anyway—was that he'd find all that out for himself soon enough.

"I just don't want you to have unrealistically high expectations of me," she said.

"Which, put in simple English, means...?"

"I don't want to disappoint you."

"No way you could do that," he told her.

"How can you know that?" she returned. "You don't really know me." Even now, there were things about herself she couldn't share with him, although she'd let him see more than she let most people see.

"Then let me get to know you." Recognizing the look on her face, he said, "Is it really that frightening a proposition?"

"Not for you maybe..."

"Yes, for me. I don't want to disappoint you, either, you know."

She smiled wryly. "We sound like a real pair of misfits, don't we?"

"Consider it something we both have in common," he noted with a grin. "Fear."

"I don't know," she mused. "I have a hard time seeing you as being afraid of anything."

"Then we're even, because I've got a hard time seeing you as anything but self-confident," he replied.

"Goes to show you how wrong you can be about someone, I guess."

"Does it feel like there's anything wrong about us?" he asked.

"No," she said softly. "It feels so right, it's scary."

"Ditto."

"Is that why you acted so coolly after you kissed me at your warehouse? Because you were scared?"

"Scared spitless," he admitted readily. "My irritating younger brother had just pointed out how laughable the idea of you and I ever getting together was."

"Laughable?" she repeated with a frown. "Your younger brother must have a strange sense of humor."

"It runs in the family. And I gotta say, he had a point. You drive a car that costs more than his house does."

"Does that bother you?"

"Not when I'm with you. But then I can't think straight when I'm with you."

Laura knew the feeling. That was how she felt whenever she was around him.

"I don't know about you, but I'm new to this kind of situation," he admitted. "I guess we'll have to give it some time and see how it goes. What do you say we try this whole thing over again? Tomorrow night. For a *real* date."

"I work tomorrow night," she said regretfully.

"How about Tuesday night, then?"

"Okay."

"Okay." Hearing the chimes sounding on the grandfather clock in the foyer, Sam reluctantly got up. "You were right. It is getting late. And we've both got to get up early tomorrow.'' He held his hand out to her. "Walk me to the door.''

"You mean the door with the great hardware?'' she asked teasingly.

"Not the best opening line, was it?'' He twined his fingers around hers. "I'll try to do better Tuesday night. Maybe I should bring flowers instead of wine.''

"Oh, my gosh!'' She put her hand to her mouth. "I forgot all about the wine you brought.''

"That's probably just as well,'' he said. "I feel drunk enough as it is.'' He trailed his fingers over the curve of her cheek. "You appear to have that kind of effect on me.''

"I'm afraid the feeling is mutual,'' she confessed unsteadily.

"Good.'' He couldn't resist giving her one final brief kiss. "Sleep tight. I'll pick you up at six Tuesday night.''

Laura closed the door after him and leaned against it, unable to believe that an evening that had started out so wrong could have ended up so right!

"So, how'd your evening with Sam go?'' Hazel asked the second Laura walked into the office Monday morning. "Did you follow my advice?''

"Don't I always follow your advice, Hazel?''

"No. You're not going to tell me, are you?'' she said with resignation.

"That's right,'' Laura confirmed.

"Is that any way to treat your faithful receptionist?''

"It's the best way to treat my wonderfully talented receptionist.''

Hazel shook her head. "I wonder if Sam's secretary had any better luck with him than I'm having with you.'' She reached for the phone. "Maybe I should call her and find out.''

"Don't you dare!" Laura warned, sighing with relief when Hazel removed her hand from the phone. "Do you really know his secretary?"

"Oh, yes. Quite well."

"What's she like?" Laura asked with what she hoped was casual interest.

"An exotic beauty with the hots for Sam."

Laura almost dropped the mail she was looking through. "What!"

Hazel grinned. "Just testing. Actually she's been working for Mitchell and Sons longer than Sam's been alive. That gives her an unfair advantage over me. She's developed her own way of getting information out of Sam that I haven't had time to develop with you yet."

Laura couldn't help wondering what Sam was telling Mabel, if he was telling her anything. The woman sounded pretty intimidating, but then Sam was no novice when it came to getting what he wanted—she could vouch for that!

Across town in his office, Sam was eyeing Mabel with reluctant admiration and genuine irritation. She had determination, he'd give her that much. But he wouldn't give her any of the details she was trying to pry out of him about his evening with Laura.

"Mabel, we've both got a lot of work to get through before I go out to tour that old theater site this morning, so what do you say we skip the rest of the inquisition and get back to work."

"Fine." She folded her arms across her chest. "The sooner you answer my question, the sooner we can get to work."

"You don't seem to understand. *I'm* the boss. *You're* the secretary. I'm supposed to give the orders. You're supposed to obey them."

Mabel snorted. "That'll be the day."

Sam frowned at her. "Were you this difficult with my dad?"

"Your dad and I had a perfect understanding. Still do. *You're* the one giving *me* a hard time."

"Now, Mabel, I can't believe you don't have anything better to do than to speculate about my activities."

"I got plenty of better things to do."

"Good. Then go do them," he said. "Starting with the letters I just dictated."

Mabel's expression changed from belligerence to long-suffering forbearance. "Can I help it if I worry about you?"

"What's there to worry about?" he demanded.

"That you might get your heart broken by some highfa-lutin lady dentist."

He grinned at her reassuringly. "Hey, Mabel, my heart's shatterproof, you should know that by now."

"Sure. That's what you'd like everyone to think, but some of us know better."

Something about the way she said that made him suspicious. "Have you been talking with my mom by any chance?" One look at her face was all he needed for confirmation. "I thought so."

Mabel returned to her formerly bristling posture. "It's only natural for a mother to be worried when a son who shows no sign of settling down suddenly takes after a strange woman."

"I'm not taking after her, and she's not strange, Mabel."

"Then why are you so secretive about her?" she demanded.

Sam rolled his eyes in exasperation. "Listen, the minute I hear wedding bells ringing, you and my mom will be the first to know, okay! Until then, would you please get off my back!"

"What's this about wedding bells?" Frank asked as he and Joey entered the office.

"Hey, bro, don't tell me you're even thinking of trading in your carefree existence for a ball and chain," Joey said in dismay.

"I'm thinking of trading in my entire family," Sam retorted. "The entire busybody lot of you. Did I ever put you guys through the third degree when you were single?"

"Yes," Frank and Joey said in unison.

"And you're not going to let me forget it, are you?"

"Nope," they both replied.

"We haven't had this much fun teasing you since you split your pants at your eighth-grade graduation party," Frank said.

"One of the personal highlights of my life, I'm sure," Sam observed dryly. "Excuse me if I leave you two meatheads to reminisce over old times, but some of us have work to do and I'm already late for a meeting."

"You don't think he's really serious about this lady dentist, do you?" Joey asked Mabel as soon as Sam had gone.

"And what if he is?" Mabel said in a surprising turnabout. "Don't you know it's impolite to go butting into other people's lives? Some people don't know when to mind their own business," she huffed before marching back to her desk.

Laura couldn't figure it out. She'd been looking forward to her date with Sam. But now that he was ringing her doorbell, she was suddenly having second thoughts—not about going out with him, but about dating. The social ritual didn't conjure up many pleasant associations for her.

When the bell rang again, she opened the door. Standing there was an unfamiliar-looking Sam, wearing an honest-to-goodness suit. He looked as ill at ease as she felt.

"Hi," he said.

"Hi," she parroted.

"Are you ready to go?"

"Yes."

It wasn't until he'd helped her into his well-kept vintage Mustang and had gone around to sit in the driver's seat that Sam spoke again.

"Do you feel as stupid as I do?" he demanded irritably.

"More."

"Impossible."

"No, it's not," she assured him.

"This is ridiculous. What are we so nervous about?"

"I think maybe it's the term 'date.' It makes you feel that you have to be on your best behavior."

"Then maybe we should cut right to the part where we get to make out in the car," Sam suggested with a look that was positively wicked.

To his surprise she said, "Maybe we should." He was about to move closer when she added the clincher. "That is, if you don't mind the members of the Women's Sewing League looking on. They're all on my neighbor's front porch."

"Damn!" he muttered in frustration. The sewing league wasn't nicknamed "The Snoop Sisters" for nothing.

"Sam Mitchell, is that you?" Mrs. Witherspoon called out from the porch. "Say hi to your mom for me."

Sam hoped his grimace would pass for a smile, but just in case it wouldn't, he added a wave out the window as he hurriedly backed the Mustang out of the driveway.

He didn't stop until they reached the stoplight on Main Street, which happened to be red. Then he stole a look at Laura, who was stealing a look at him. A second later they were both laughing.

"Ah, the dangers of small-town living," Sam declared. "Everybody either knows or wants to know everybody else's business."

Laura nodded. "You can say that again. I got the third degree from Hazel yesterday."

"You're not the only one. Our secretary, Mabel, has perfected interrogation to a fine art."

"Did you know that Hazel and Mabel know each other?"

Sam groaned. "The two of them get together and we won't have a chance in hell."

"Somehow I had the impression that *we* were the bosses."

"That's just what they let us think. The fact is, they know where all the files are."

"True, very true," Laura admitted. "See? Here's something else we both have in common. We both have to contend with overbearing secretaries. Doesn't make us sound like we have much gumption, though, does it?"

"Listen, General Patton himself wouldn't have much gumption against *my* secretary," Sam declared.

"Despite your complaints it sounds like you have a soft spot for her."

"Bite your tongue. But enough about me. What about you?"

"What about me?" she said.

"You know a lot more about me than I know about you. I'll bet Hazel has filled you in on my life story since the day I was born. Unfortunately I can't question anyone but you about your past."

"It's not very interesting," she replied.

"It is to me. I'll make it easy on you and start with the simple questions first. What made you want to become a dentist?"

There were a lot of reasons—some she could tell him, some she couldn't. How could she explain the need for security to someone who thought she'd been born with a silver spoon in her mouth? And telling him the entire truth about the realities of her past required a trust she was still trying to develop.

It wasn't easy. Letting go of her carefully constructed image would be like appearing naked in public, because her veneer was simply that—a veneer. She hadn't been that way all her life. It wasn't the real her.

"Hey, if it takes you this long to answer the easy questions, I hate to think what you're gonna do with the hard ones," he teased her.

Her mind returned to his original question. "It's not that easy to answer. There were so many reasons why I became a dentist. I wanted to help people, particularly children. That's why, after I graduated from dental school, I took the extra two years of graduate training required to become a pediatric dentist."

"Let me put it this way. What do you like *best* about being a dentist?"

"The smiles."

"Your patients smile?" Sam questioned in disbelief. "What do you do to them? Give them laughing gas? Tickle them with your torture tools?"

"Actually we have nicknamed one of the instruments 'the Tickler.'"

"I don't know, Laura. Sounds pretty kinky to me."

"Somehow that doesn't surprise me," she retorted.

"Just for that crack, I've got another question for you. What's the *worst* part of being a dentist?"

"The pain," she immediately replied. "And not being able to separate yourself from it. Empathizing too much. It's the reason a lot of dentists get burnout. But there is good news. Thanks to things like fluoridated water, fluoride toothpaste and plastic sealants, about half of the children under twelve in this country are cavity-free."

"Wait a second. Won't that put you out of a job?"

"Children's teeth will always need looking after, even if it's only preventive work. Then there will always be the kids who knock their teeth out—"

Sam groaned. "Do you mind? We're about to have dinner."

Their conversation was briefly put on hold as they arrived at the restaurant. But Sam resumed his questioning once they'd finished ordering. "So, you sailed through dental school—with straight A's, I'll bet. Then what did you do?"

"I wouldn't call it sailing exactly," she corrected him. "Dog-paddling is more like it."

There it was again, he noticed, that defensiveness whenever he mentioned her being smart. "If I didn't know better, I'd say you're as upset at being called smart as you were when I said you were cute. You're both, you know," he declared. "No two ways about it."

"The expert has spoken, hmm?"

"You got that right. I've got a smart brother. I recognize brains when I see them."

"Only one of your brothers is smart?"

Sam nodded. "Frank's the only one who went to college."

"What about you? Aren't you smart?"

"Me? Hey, I'm brilliant. Didn't make it to college, though."

"Does that bother you?" she asked him.

"Does it bother *you*?" he countered.

"No. Why should it?"

He shrugged. "You're the one with all the fancy degrees on your wall."

And the self-doubts in my closet, she added to herself. But it looked as if she weren't the only one. "And you're the one who's just fine the way he is," she assured him.

"The expert has spoken, hmm?"

"You got that right," she drawled, trying to imitate his accent.

"Hey, not bad. We'll have you saying your *r*'s like a true New Englander in no time."

Their conversation halted temporarily as the waitress brought the house specialty, crab, and they both dug in with their forks.

"See, I told you this would be a good idea," Sam said. "It's hard to be formal when you're eating crab. Here, you've got some butter on your chin." Leaning over, he dabbed at the spot with a paper napkin. It was meant to be a casual gesture, but it ended up being laced with intimacy as his fingers brushed over her lips.

The intensity of her feelings caught Laura by surprise, and she instinctively backed away from them, and from him.

Sam frowned. "Something wrong?"

"No, it's just . . ." She shrugged. "I'm a bit new to this."

"To eating crab?"

"Among other things."

He grinned knowingly. "Never been seduced in a restaurant before, huh?"

"Not in Massachusetts, no."

"We'll have to change that."

"You already have."

Sam had just pulled into her driveway when the yawn Laura had been fighting off for the past few minutes refused to be smothered any longer. "I'm sorry," she quickly apologized. "It's not the company. It's just that I haven't gotten much sleep the past few nights."

"Oh?" Sam switched off the ignition and turned to face her. "Why not?"

"I don't know. Maybe it's got something to do with the leaky faucet in my bathroom that keeps dripping all night long. And maybe it's got something to do with you."

"Me? What did I do?"

"Kissed me at the warehouse and then acted like it never happened."

He looked rather pleased at the news. In fact, he looked downright delighted. "So I've been keeping you up nights, have I?"

His reaction irked her somewhat. "You *and* the leaky faucet."

As he took her hand in his, he didn't appear the least bit remorseful at being even partially responsible for her sleepless nights.

"Well," he drawled. "I guess I'm gonna have to do something to fix this situation."

"What exactly are you suggesting?"

"First, that I fix your faucet." His thumb provocatively stroked the back of her hand. "We'll discuss the next step after that. I'll bring my tools over first thing Sunday morning. You should be prepared to assist me in whatever—" he wiggled his eyebrows à la Groucho Marx "—way possible."

"I'll do what I can," she assured him, trying not to laugh.

"Really? Hey, if I'm on a roll with suggestions here, how about going out dancing Saturday night?"

"Fine."

"Great. And as for the leaky faucet, I'll be at your place bright and early Sunday morning with blowtorch in hand."

"Blowtorch! Isn't that a little extreme?"

"Don't worry about a thing. You've got the right man for the job," Sam assured her with a jaunty grin.

When she opened her door on Sunday, the right-man-for-the-job was indeed standing on her doorstep, toolbox in hand. But was it really Sam? At first glance, she couldn't be sure. The man was wearing a Boston Red Sox baseball cap tugged down so low that it blocked most of his face from view.

But once Laura ran her eyes over the black T-shirt covering his chest and then down to his trademark jeans, she knew it was Sam all right. She'd recognize that body anywhere. After all, she'd spent most of last night dreaming about it—before, during and after their Saturday evening date.

Still it was better to be safe than sorry, so she leaned closer, trying to see the face hidden in the shade of his baseball cap. "Sam, is that you?"

"Who else were you expecting?" he growled as he stepped inside. "God, it's bright out there." He dumped his red metal tool chest on the floor before taking off his baseball cap and squinting at her. "Some wild woman kept me out half the night last night and I didn't get much sleep."

"We can make it another day if you're not feeling well..." she said uncertainly.

He snared her in his arms with surprising speed. "I'll feel better once I've had a kiss and some coffee, in that order."

Laura decided she could easily get used to starting all her days this way—with his mouth nibbling hers as if she were a delicious delicacy that only came along once in a blue moon.

"I'm not a wild woman," she said demurely, despite the fact that she'd just kissed him like one. "And your eyes don't look the least bit bloodshot for a man who was out half the night."

"You must've shocked the life back into me."

"I can tell," she murmured with a provocative laugh. "I'd better go get that coffee while I still can."

"I guess you'd better." Reluctantly, he released her from his embrace and followed her into the kitchen.

"Here." She handed him a mug of freshly brewed coffee. "When you're done with that, we'll go to my bedroom."

He almost choked on his coffee. "We will?"

Laura nodded. "If that's okay with you."

"Fine. It's fine with me. Let's leave the coffee here." He set the mug down so quickly that the dark liquid splashed out onto the countertop. "I don't need any more."

"Okay."

She led him upstairs to the doorway at the end of the hallway.

Sam barely noticed the blue, pink and white color scheme of the room. His eyes were drawn to her double bed, which was neatly made.

She seemed to be looking at him expectantly, so he said, "Nice. Real nice."

"I'm not done with the decorating yet."

"Looks good to me." Damn good. He could picture the two of them on that bed, rumpling the neat covers, rumpling each other. Stripping away the bedspread, their clothes...

"The bathroom's through here," Laura said.

"Bathroom?"

"That's right. The one with the leaky faucet, remember?"

"Sure." He cleared his throat. "Sure, I remember." Seeing her grin, he gave her a reprimanding look. "You're a cruel woman, torturing me this way."

"I'm sorry," she said with such exaggerated repentance that it was clear she wasn't telling the truth. Actually, she wasn't the least bit sorry. Flirting with him had opened an entirely new world to her, and she was enjoying every minute of it. "Allow me to make it up to you," she murmured while running her fingers over his chest.

"This had better be good," he warned her, trying not to grin.

"Oh, it will be." She slipped away before his arms could encircle her. "I'll make it up to you by going downstairs to get your toolbox for you. For some reason you left it down there. I can't imagine why..." Her voice trailed off as she tossed him a jaunty smile over her shoulder before she left.

"Well, I can imagine why," he called after her. "And I can imagine plenty of better ways for you to make it up to me."

"Good." Her voice floated upstairs to him. "I like a man with a little imagination."

"My imagination is not little!" he shouted down to her.

"I apologize again. Let me rephrase that statement," she said as she reentered the bedroom with his toolbox in hand. "What I meant was I like a man with a *sexy* imagination."

"That's better."

"Of course, a man with a sexy imagination *and* a toolbox—now that's an irresistible combination. What have you got in this thing anyway?" she asked as she set the box on the bathroom floor. "It weighs a ton."

"Oh, not much. Just a few tools of the trade for us guys with sexy imaginations. You know. Whips, chains, that sort of thing."

"What?" She looked over his shoulder as he opened the clasp on the box. "No black leather?"

"Why, Dr. Peters! I'm beginning to see you in an entirely different light," he said, eyeing her with rueful admiration.

"That's the fluorescent lighting," she retorted.

"No, it's not. It's you. Amazing me. I sure hope I haven't bitten off more than I can chew."

"With the sink?"

"With you, lady. With you."

"Oh, I think you underestimate yourself. I think you'll be able to handle whatever comes your way. With the sink or with me. Now," she said briskly, "shall we get to work?"

Two hours later they were still hard at work. Sam was lying on his back, spread-eagled on her bathroom floor. His head and shoulders were hidden under the sink cabinet while an array of tools were scattered around him.

"Pipe wrench." He held his hand out the way a surgeon would.

"What does it look like?" Laura asked.

"The blue thing."

She handed it to him as she'd been handing him tools all morning. In between admiring his body, that was. She couldn't help herself. Besides, he couldn't tell where she was looking; he had his head stuck under the sink basin. She'd propped several pillows on the floor so that he could lie there comfortably...while she sat next him and gazed to her heart's content. He should wear jeans and black T-shirts all the time, she decided.

"Laura!"

She jumped guiltily. "What?"

"The basin wrench."

"Oh. Sorry. Which one is that?"

"It's got a long stalk, and on top—a funny alligator-looking thing that swivels."

His description was appropriate, and she had no problem picking out the tool. "Here." She placed it in his hand. "How is it going?"

"Fine." His voice was muffled by the sink cabinet.

"Can I get you some iced tea?" she asked him.

"Sounds good."

She welcomed the opportunity to get away for a minute. It was getting hot in the small bathroom, in more ways than one. Having his muscular body spread out on the bathroom floor that way was giving her ideas—sexy ideas.

When she returned a short while later with two tall glasses of iced tea, her thoughts were steamier than Sam's language as he swore at a wrench.

Kneeling next to him, she put her hand on his stomach to signal her return. "I brought your tea."

"Thanks. Just put it over there. I'll drink it in a minute. Could you hand me a rag from the toolbox?"

"Sure." She had to lean over him to reach it.

"All right, that does it!" He sat up so quickly she ended up half-sitting in his lap. Although he was glaring at her, there was no mistaking the gleam in his brown eyes. "I can't take it any longer! Don't try giving me that innocent look, you know exactly what I'm talking about. Those little touches, brushing against me—"

"I was only trying to reach the toolbox," she protested. "I think you deliberately placed it where I had to lean over you to get to it."

"Damn right I did!" he readily admitted. "I'm no dummy."

"And you've got the nerve to accuse *me* of being distracting?" She gently punched his shoulder, which felt as solid as granite. "What about you? If I brushed against you, you brushed against me twice as much."

"Did not!"

"Did, too!"

They grinned at each other.

Then, seeing the way she was gleefully eyeing his rib cage, Sam said, "Don't even think about it. Laura, I'm warning you..."

She didn't pay any attention to him and tickled him anyway, watching in delight as he doubled over and wiggled to get away. It took him a few seconds, but he eventually managed to clamp his hands around her wrists. "Okay, lady, you asked for it."

This time Laura was the one to start scooting away. "Now, Sam..."

"Don't 'Now, Sam' me. You tickled a defenseless man when he was down. That calls for serious action."

She leaned closer and slipped in another tickle, which enabled her to make her getaway. She didn't get very far, though. With the roar of a mighty hunter, Sam chased after her.

"Gotcha!" he said triumphantly before tumbling them both onto her bed. "Now what have you got to say for yourself?"

Laura suddenly lacked the presence of mind, or the oxygen, to say anything at all. Pressed against him, she could feel every inch of his body. Suddenly laughter was replaced with something equally exhilarating. Passion.

He felt it, too. The hunger and the promise. The desire to act instead of tease. It was all there in his eyes. That and more.

She was powerless to resist. Yet in that moment she felt more powerful than she'd ever felt before. She was the one who'd made him feel this way, who'd made him look this way.

Once their mouths met, any hope of restraint fled beneath the wildfire of need. She was unprepared for the heat. For the scalding pleasure. Faster. Hotter. She could scarcely breathe. She didn't care. Kissing him and being kissed by him was more essential than breathing. She didn't need oxygen; she needed him.

And he needed her. She could feel how much as he rocked against her, letting her know the strength of his desire. She wanted to be closer to him. Impatient of the barriers still between them, Laura slipped her hands beneath his T-shirt. His bare skin was warm beneath her fingertips.

Sam responded by unbuttoning her blouse and then undoing her bra with an urgency she welcomed. She wanted to feel his hands on her as much as he wanted to touch her. *More.*

She didn't realize she'd spoken the word aloud until Sam repeated it, his voice as ragged as hers. She closed her eyes as he lowered his lips, shifting his attention from the corner of her mouth to the hollow of her throat. Murmuring his appreciation, he cupped her breast with the palm of his hand. Laura was trembling with excitement. When his lips tugged at the hardened peak, she thought she'd die. Her fingers fanned out into his dark hair as she held him closer.

Sam lifted his head and looked down at her. Her eyes were closed, her face flushed. This was the way he'd imagined her—warm and willing.

Laura opened her eyes and returned his gaze. This was the way she'd imagined him—tender and seductive.

No words were spoken. None were needed. Sam smiled. So did Laura. And then his mouth returned to hers, moving over her lips with an unhurried sensuality.

Pounding. Loud. Relentless. Her heart or his? Laura wondered with hazy curiosity. No, it was the door. Someone pounding on her front door.

"It's okay," Sam whispered. "Ignore them, and they'll go away."

The pounding didn't go away. It got louder.

"I'll go get rid of them," Sam declared, intensely frustrated by the interruption.

She held him back. "No." She sat up, hurriedly refastening her bra and her blouse as she did so. It helped that the blouse didn't have many buttons, because her fingers were less than steady. "I'll go. I'll be right back."

"Don't forget." He gave her a sizzling kiss to remind her. "Get rid of them. Fast."

"I will," she promised.

But when she got downstairs she discovered Jerry pounding on her front door, shouting that he needed to talk to her.

She opened the door. "What is it? What's wrong?"

"It's my wife. She's left me!"

"Oh, Jerry..."

"I don't know what to do." He grabbed her arm. "You've got to help me!"

Laura bit her lip as she looked from Jerry's desperate face to the stairway leading up to the bedroom. She didn't see that she had much choice here. She couldn't simply close the door in Jerry's face.

"Try to stay calm and just tell me what happened."

"I got home and found this note." Jerry shoved the crumpled piece of paper at her. "There. Read it for yourself."

Laura tried to, but his wife's handwriting was hard to decipher. Growing impatient, Jerry grabbed the note back again. "I'll read it for you.

"Dear Jerry, I've gone away to think things over. We don't seem to have much of a life left together. You probably won't even miss me."

Jerry held back a sob. "Laura, what am I going to do?"

She patted him on the shoulder with one hand while handing him a Kleenex with the other. "Do you have any idea where she might have gone?"

He nodded. "To her mother's house in Boston."

"Maybe you should go after her."

"You think she wants me to?"

"You know her better than I do, Jerry. What do you think?"

"I don't know what to think. I can't believe this is happening to me. I didn't see this coming at all. I'm sorry about bursting in here, but . . ." His voice cracked as tears came to his eyes.

"That's all right." Leaning closer, she put her arm around his shoulder in a gesture of commiseration. "I wish I could do more to help."

To Sam, coming down the stairs, Laura and her "just friends" dental partner looked very cozy indeed. The two of them were standing there, heads together, sharing secrets.

He'd heard the low pitch of their voices from the bedroom and had decided to come see what was taking Laura so long to get rid of the unwelcome intruder. Here was his answer. The intruder wasn't unwelcome after all. Sam was the one who felt like an intruder. His presence clearly wasn't required here.

Laura looked up to see him standing on the stairs, the expression on his face so cold and remote that she actually shivered.

Without saying a word, he headed for the front door as if shot out of a cannon.

Startled, Laura hurried after him. "Sam, wait!"

"Sink's fixed." He threw the curt words at her over his shoulder as he continued on his way to his car without breaking stride. A second later he and his Mustang were gone.

Six

———

"Did I interrupt something?" Jerry asked once Laura had returned inside and closed the door.

What could she say? Jerry was in bad enough shape without her adding any more guilt. "No, you didn't interrupt," she murmured.

"So what do you think I should do about Trish?"

Laura forced herself to refocus her attention on Jerry. "Trish? Right. Well, I think you should call her at her mother's and talk to her, see how she feels, let her know how you feel. Tell her that you love her."

"You think so?"

"Yes." She talked with Jerry for another twenty minutes before he began to feel better.

"Thanks for the pep talk," he said. "I'm going to go home and call Trish right now. And I'm sorry about barging in the way I did. I think I did interrupt something."

"Don't worry about it." She still couldn't believe Sam had walked out the way he had.

As soon as she was alone, Laura threw herself down onto the couch Sam had eyed so warily a week ago. Like her, the couch was actually more sensible than it first appeared to be. Sure it looked daintily elegant with its plush velour upholstery, but it was built like a rock. Comfortable, too. Otherwise she wouldn't have bought it.

She lay there, glumly staring at the hole in her left sock, and wondered why she was comparing herself to a couch when her relationship with Sam was in deep trouble. Trivializing, the medical student in her said. Common reaction to emotional stress.

"Oh, shut up," she muttered to that voice in her head. Then she began her pep talk. "Okay, this is not a problem. You can handle this. Just phone Sam and ask him what the hell he thought he was doing walking out that way. Only word it politely. Stay calm," she added as she sat up and reached for the phone.

She was ready. Only Sam wasn't home, or at least there was no answer to her call.

She slammed the phone down. "If that's the way he wants to be about it...fine! He's the one who walked out. He's the one who can call me."

Sam didn't call, but he did come knocking on her door later that afternoon—looking only slightly less remote than he had when he'd left several hours earlier, which wasn't a good sign, in her opinion. Still, he *had* come.

"I've decided to let you explain what was going on here earlier," he stated magnanimously.

Laura couldn't believe her ears. "How generous of you," she retorted, stung by his incredible bullheadedness. "For your information, nothing was going on!" She was so angry, she turned away and left him standing on her front porch.

He didn't stay there long. "What do you mean nothing was going on?" he demanded, slamming the door behind him as he followed her into her living room. "That's not how it looked to me."

"Then you need to have your vision tested!"

"Listen, all I know is that things were going real well between us when you left, promising you'd get rid of whoever was at the door. I stayed there waiting for you to come back, and when you didn't, I came downstairs to find you practically hugging Jerry."

"I wasn't hugging him, practically or otherwise."

"Well, you certainly weren't trying to get rid of him," Sam accused.

"His wife just left him. What did you want me to say? 'Have your nervous breakdown later, Jerry, it's not convenient for me right now'?"

"I thought you said the two of you were just friends and business partners."

"We are."

"Then why were you hugging him? Why did he come to you as soon as his wife left him?"

"Because he was a basket case and I am a friend. Jerry loves his wife very much. Her leaving him without warning this way has shaken him. And under those conditions I couldn't just shove him back out the door. As for hugging him, I had my hand on his shoulder, that's all. But even if I had been hugging him, that was no excuse for your behavior."

"Let me get this straight," Sam said. "You expect me to just stand by while you're—"

"While I'm giving a good friend a little human kindness when he's suffered a great shock. Yes, I do expect that of you, Sam. At the very least, I expect you to get the facts straight before you go running off."

"Seeing the two of you together that way, what else was I to think?"

"You actually believe I'd be as close to you as I was upstairs in my room and then come downstairs to fool around with another man?"

Sam shifted uncomfortably. "Of course I don't think that. I wasn't thinking clearly at the time. Okay, I wasn't thinking at all. Does that make you happy?"

"Not really."

"I made a mistake. So shoot me."

"Don't think I wasn't tempted when you first walked in here," she snapped.

"You both looked so right together, like a matched set or something. He looked like he'd just come off a golf course, and you looked—"

"Like I'd been rolling around in bed with you," Laura inserted. "Jerry could tell something was up."

"Did you tell him about us?"

"Sam, his wife just left him. I didn't think the time was appropriate to be discussing my romantic relationships."

"But you do plan on telling him?" he persisted in asking.

"I don't know."

"That's just great," Sam muttered in disgust, his anger rising again. "Why don't you want Jerry knowing that you're seeing me? Because I'm not good enough? Because you're ashamed of me?"

"I've never been ashamed of you!" she vehemently denied. "I was embarrassed by the situation, not by being with you. And what exactly was I supposed to say to Jerry? Sam and I were upstairs fooling around? We're seeing each other? We're dating? You see? *I* don't even know what to call what we're doing," she declared in exasperation.

"But we sure were having fun doing it, you have to admit that much."

Just as he'd hoped, she smiled, albeit reluctantly.

"Okay," she said. "I'll admit that much. To you. But not to Jerry or the rest of Baileys Crossing."

"This is a small town," he reminded her. "It's hard to keep secrets here for long. Why do you want to?"

"Because I don't find it very easy to share my deepest emotions with everyone. I'm not comfortable announcing my feelings to the world. Or even to Baileys Crossing."

"How about to me?" he asked. "Are you comfortable announcing your feelings to me?"

"I'm working on it. What we've got...it's something special, Sam. Or at least it feels that way to me."

"Feels that way to me, too."

"And being special I want to keep it to myself for a little while longer. Can you understand that?"

"I suppose so."

"Believe me," Laura said. "It's got nothing to do with me being ashamed of you. I mean, it's not like I'm trying to sweep you under a rug and hide you there. Hazel knows we're seeing each other. So does Mabel. So half the town probably knows it."

"Why does that bother you so much?"

"Because even though I've lived here almost three years, I haven't gotten used to my private life being so public. As the outsider here, I'm still trying to fit in."

"You're not an outsider. Well, maybe you are a little bit," he admitted, "but then so is everyone who wasn't born here. That doesn't mean you're not well liked or well thought of by the people here. Because you are. *Very* well liked. *Very* well thought of." He snared her in his arms. "Especially by me."

As Sam moved in to kiss her, she put her hand on his chest to stop him. "Wait. If you start kissing me again, I won't be able to think straight. And there's something else I have to say."

Sam sighed impatiently. "Now what?" he asked with fatalistic resignation.

"It might have been a good thing that Jerry stopped by when he did. It's too soon for us to... I mean, things were moving pretty fast there."

"I don't know about that." Sam trailed his fingers down her back. "Some of those moves were pretty slow, as I recall."

"It's just... I don't think we should rush into anything."

"Into bed, you mean."

"To put it bluntly, yes."

"We're going to end up making love, Laura. It's simply a matter of time."

She stepped away from him but didn't disagree with him. This was a time for honesty. "Look, there's something you should know about me. I haven't exactly had a lot of experience with this sort of thing. I'm not even sure I'm really good at it," she muttered.

"Trust me," he said. "You're damn good at it."

"Thanks, I think. But the truth is that... You see how it is with me?" she exclaimed with exasperation. "I get all tongue-tied talking about things this personal."

"So what?"

"So I sound like an idiot."

"Not to me you don't. You sound human. Something wrong with that?" Sam inquired.

"You don't seem to have this problem."

"Ah, but then you don't hear me talking about my past, do you?"

"I'm sure that if and when you do, it'll be with a lot more competence than I seem to be displaying."

"The presentation isn't important, Laura. The content is. Just tell me what you want to say."

She tried to choose her words carefully. "There haven't been many men in my life. Two to be exact. One I went with all through college." What she didn't say was that Andrew had been her first lover, her only lover. "The second relationship wasn't quite as serious and certainly didn't last as long. He was a suave charmer. I was a challenge. It didn't work out." Because she'd found out, in the nick of time, that the man in question had a fiancée waiting at home.

"So? I don't get the connection. What does that have to do with us? *I've* never been to college and I sure ain't suave," he drawled.

"You are a charmer, though."

"What am I supposed to say to that?" he countered somewhat impatiently. "Deny it and sound modest? Acknowledge it and sound conceited? If I were a real charmer I'd know the right thing to say here, and I sure as hell don't."

"Say you'll be patient."

"I'll be patient," he stated solemnly, and then grinned wickedly. "You don't have to make love with me this afternoon. Tomorrow will do."

"That wasn't exactly what I meant by patient," she returned ruefully.

"Hey, I can't promise that I won't try to change your mind. But I can promise that I won't do anything to hurt you. That I won't dump you just because you said no this time. Good enough for you?"

She nodded. "Thanks."

"You're welcome. See? Your good manners must be rubbing off on me. Got me thinking about formal invitations and all that stuff. So, Dr. Peters, I'd like to take this opportunity to formally invite you to come with me to the Easter parade next Saturday. And your formal reply is?"

"That I'm one step ahead of you."

"You are?"

She nodded. "I was going to invite *you* to help with the Easter egg hunt in the park before the parade. I'm in charge of the event this year. It would mean getting to the park's community center at seven in the morning and staying there until the parade begins. I thought you might like to volunteer to help me," she suggested hopefully.

Sam groaned. "Surrounded by rug rats? What could be worse?"

"Don't give me that," she chided him. "I know you like kids."

"Where did you get an idea like that?"

"From the way you acted with your niece."

"That was nothing. No one likes to see a kid tortured."

"Or frightened? Or lonely?"

He shifted uncomfortably. "It was no big deal."

"Coming to a place you hate because your niece needed you? I think it was sweet," she said.

He grimaced.

"Now you know how I felt when you called me cute," she told him with a grin.

"So you were just trying to pay me back, huh? Sneaky. You're a sneaky, sexy, classy, cute lady."

"And you're a sweet guy who's going to bring his own basket for the Easter egg hunt."

"I thought only kids were allowed to participate."

"Who said anything about participating? You're going to help me hide the Easter eggs."

"I am?"

"Aren't you?" she countered.

His reply was issued in the form of a warning. "Just don't expect me to dress up in any bunny costume."

On the Saturday before Easter, Sam was standing in the community center, staring at Laura as if she'd taken leave

of her senses. "No way! You can't be serious! I told you—
no bunny costume!"

"I know. I didn't plan it this way, honest. But Smitty got
sick at the last minute, and you're the only one I could think
of to replace him."

"Smitty from Lucky Liquor?"

She nodded.

"He's not sick. He's hung over the same way he is every
Saturday morning after his bimonthly Friday-night poker
game. Whose dumb idea was it to have him be the Easter
bunny anyway?"

"Mine."

"Oh."

"No one else seemed to think there would be a problem
having Smitty be the Easter bunny," she said defensively.

"Yeah, well not everyone knows about Smitty's poker-
playing-and-drinking binges," Sam admitted. "Which goes
to show you that, despite what you think about Baileys
Crossing, everyone here doesn't know *everything* about
everyone else."

"That's irrelevant at the moment. Now we have to worry
about getting you into this costume."

"No, we don't. I'm not wearing that thing," he declared
adamantly. "So you can just put it right back in the box."

"Come on, Sam," she coaxed him. "Be a good sport."

"No way."

"Think of all those kids out there waiting for the Easter
bunny to show up."

He was unmoved. "Get someone else to do the job." He
pointed a finger out the window where a crowd had gathered in the adjacent park. "You can't tell me there aren't
plenty of guys out there, or women, either, for that matter,
who couldn't be an Easter bunny and do a much better job
at it than I could."

"There isn't time to go find someone. Besides, most of those adults out there are parents and they've got kids of their own to take care of. Kids who might notice their parents' absence and recognize them as the Easter bunny."

"So get someone who's not a parent. No way I'm the only single person in Baileys Crossing."

"You're the only one here this early in the morning for a 'kids only' Easter egg hunt. Aside from me, that is. And if you won't dress up in the costume, then I guess I'll have to."

"Fine. You wear it."

"Fine," Laura retorted. "I will."

She grabbed the oversize costume and, moving so that she couldn't be seen from the window, tugged it on over her jeans and T-shirt.

Sam took one look at her lost in the folds of material and rolled his eyes in exasperation.

"Here, give it to me," he muttered. "Just don't let anyone know it's me," he warned her as she peeled off the costume and handed it to him with great delight.

"I won't. Thanks. I owe you one."

"Yes, you do. And don't think I'm not gonna collect," he said, giving her a brief but blistering kiss before sending her out the door. "Go stall the kids for me. I'll be out there in five minutes."

"Won't you need help getting into the costume?"

"No, it zips up the front, thank God. I feel dumb enough walking around in this thing without having you watch me. Go on," he told her. "Before I change my mind."

Afterward the kids said that this year's Easter bunny was one of the best ever.

"You got rave reviews," Laura told Sam, wishing she'd had more of a chance to see his performance herself, but she'd been busy supervising the Easter egg hunt.

"Yeah, well just don't expect an encore. You wouldn't believe some of the things those kids said to me... I mean, said to the Easter bunny."

"Really? Like what?"

"Like, 'Would you take my sister back? I don't want her around anymore.' Like, 'I want a hundred dollar bill in my Easter egg.' And there was one kid, Tommy Maloney, who wouldn't keep his hands off my cottontail."

"It's amazing you made it out alive," she said with what she hoped was the proper amount of awe.

"It's amazing that Maloney kid made it out alive," Sam muttered with a dark scowl. "Let's get out of here."

"What's the hurry?" she asked as he rushed her down the steps of the park's white-frame gazebo, where earlier she and Sam had hidden plenty of brightly colored plastic Easter eggs—all of which had been found by excited little hands.

"The hurry is that I don't want to miss the Easter bonnet contest and the chance to see my brother Frank making a fool of himself. He's entered in the 'most outlandish' category. Wait till you get a load of his hat. Talk about far-out. It's a cross between one of those beer-drinking, couch-potato models—you know the ones, complete with beer can and drinking straws attached to the hat? Anyway, it's a cross between that and Darth Vader's black mask from *Star Wars*."

"Sounds interesting, but I've got to stop off at home and change before I do anything else."

Sam checked his watch. "All right, we've got just enough time to do that."

"What's with the *we*? You don't have to come with me," Laura said. "I can change and meet you back here."

"No way. Who knows? You might need help fastening something. Or unfastening it."

"I've been getting dressed on my own for thirty-one years now, Sam. I think I can manage by myself."

"Yes, but managing isn't much fun. Especially by yourself."

"Sure you don't need any help?" he asked again once they entered her house.

"Positive. You—" she pointed at his chest "—wait down here."

Sam held her hand against his heart, letting her feel its increased rhythm as he kissed her. They were both smiling when he released her.

"Five minutes," he yelled up after her. "Then I'm coming to get you!"

"Don't even think about it!" she yelled back.

"Oh, I'll think about it," he murmured, and had great fun doing so, but he stayed downstairs even though she took ten minutes instead of five.

Her flowery dress was definitely worth the extra wait, he decided. "Nice. Very nice."

"Thanks. Although I'll have you know that I ruined a perfectly good pair of stockings trying to rush because of you," she grumbled.

"I'll make it up to you," he promised with a seductive smile. "But not right now. We don't want to miss—"

She laughed. "I know, I know. We don't want to miss Frank making a fool of himself."

"Exactly."

They made the trip back to the park in record time, with Laura practically having to jog to keep up with Sam.

"Sure you don't want to enter the bonnet contest?" he asked her. "There's still time."

"That's okay." She shook her head at some of the contestants walking by—including the proud owner of a model with a teddy-bear head on top of it. "I'm not the outlandish type."

"You never know till you try. You don't always have to be classy, you know."

His comment surprised her. "I don't?"

"No."

"I'm not *always* classy. I was wearing jeans earlier."

"Sure you were wearing jeans earlier, but the first time I picked you up you were wearing fancy purple pants and a matching jacket," he reminded her.

"Until you so brilliantly pointed out that it might not be appropriate attire for crawling around under bushes hiding Easter eggs."

"Is that what I said?"

"Actually, to quote you exactly, you said, 'You can't wear that. No way.' "

"And I was right, wasn't I?" Sam said.

"Yes, but it's impolite to keep harping on it."

"Who's harping?"

"You are," she replied.

"Maybe I am, but it's hard not to tease you."

"So I've noticed." Tugging him to a sudden stop, she lowered her voice. "Don't look now, but Hazel and Mabel are standing over there looking as if they're plotting something."

"Probably our marriage."

Laura's mouth almost dropped open. "What?"

"Just kidding. Actually, Mabel's afraid you're dallying with me and will end up breaking my heart."

"Where did she ever get an idea like that?" Laura demanded.

"From my mom, maybe?"

"Oh, great," she muttered in dismay. "First your younger brother thinks a relationship between us is laughable, now your mother thinks I'm after your body."

"You mean you're not after my body?" he asked with disappointment.

"I'm serious, Sam. Why didn't you tell me that your family is against your seeing me?"

"They're not against it. But even if they were, my family doesn't control me. They just like to think they do," he added with a grin. "You'll see what I mean once you meet them."

"I don't think I'm ready for that yet."

"What? You're not eager to meet the Mitchell gang?"

"I've already met some of them," she reminded him. "Your niece is one of my patients, remember? So I already know Cindy and her mom. And I think I've seen your father a few times at historical society meetings. I may also have seen your other sister-in-law at a Friends of the Library function."

"Then you know half the family already. What's the big deal?"

"Seeing them across a crowded room and being interrogated by them are two different things," she pointed out.

"Can't argue with that," he admitted. "Okay, we'll hold off having you meet my family. For the time being."

"Thanks."

"Yet another favor I've granted you. Don't think I'm not keeping track, 'cause I am."

"I'm sure you are," she said.

"So you attend historical society and library meetings? I had no idea you were that involved with local doings."

Laura shrugged. "I like to help out where I can. It's not always an easy job for an outsider to break into a small community's groups."

"Don't let them intimidate you. Just imagine them in their underwear. I know I've done that with you." He grinned at her and wriggled his eyebrows. "Works great!"

"Not for me it doesn't. I've tried it whenever I've had to give a speech like the one I'm going to be giving in Toronto next month. It's never helped."

"Wait a minute. Back up here. What was that about your speaking in Toronto next month?"

"I'm giving a presentation at a dental convention there."

"How long will you be gone?"

"Four days. Thursday through Sunday. You won't even notice I'm gone."

"Oh, I'll notice all right." And he wasn't pleased about it.

The time for Laura's departure to Toronto came much too soon for Sam. He didn't like the thought of her being so far away from him. He knew she'd only be gone for four days, and he knew he was blowing the whole thing out of proportion. He also knew there was nothing he could do about it, except to insist that he drive her to Boston's Logan airport for her flight. At least he'd have her to himself for an extra few hours that way.

Laura, who'd been up half the night trying to cram her clothes into a shrinking suitcase, could tell as soon as he arrived to pick her up that Sam still wasn't pleased about her trip. Actually, she wasn't very pleased about it herself at the moment.

Whatever had possessed her to accept this invitation to lecture at a workshop? She must have been out of her mind. She hated making speeches. Writing an article once a month for the *Baileys Crossing Weekly News* about good dental hygiene was one thing. But these were dentists she would be talking to. Knowledgeable people. Pros.

She'd make an idiot out of herself. She'd be sick. She'd die. She'd cancel.

With her brooding about her speech and Sam brooding about her leaving, the long drive to Boston was a quiet one.

Sam didn't just drop her off at the airport as she'd half-expected him to. Instead he parked the car and came into the airport with her, questioning her as they went along.

"You've got your passport?" he asked.

"Got it."

"Boarding pass?"

"Got it."

"Return ticket?"

"Got it."

"My phone number?"

"Memorized it a long time ago."

"Going to miss me?"

If I don't get sick to my stomach first, she thought to herself with frantic anxiety as they approached the security checkpoint beyond which only passengers were allowed. The butterflies in her stomach had suddenly turned into vultures. Panicking, she reached out and grabbed Sam's hand.

"What is it?" he asked. "Did you change your mind about going?"

The hopeful way Sam posed the question brought a reluctant smile to her face. "Let's just say I'm not real eager to go," she admitted wryly.

"Great." Putting his arm around her, he guided her in an abrupt about-face. "We'll just turn around and go back to Baileys Crossing."

"Sam, I can't do that." Laughing, she tugged him to a halt. "They're expecting me in Toronto."

"I know, I know." He grinned at her. "You'll have to admit that it did sound like a tempting idea, though."

"More tempting than you can imagine," she whispered, squeezing his hand. "And to belatedly answer your question, I am going to miss you. A lot."

"Good. Now stop worrying. You're gonna knock 'em dead in Toronto. Just don't go knocking any men off their feet the way you did me."

"I won't."

"Promise?"

"Promise."

"Good."

She watched as the humor reflected in his brown eyes was replaced by passion. By desire. By need.

Laura knew she was looking at him that way, too.

It took the arrival of a bunch of jostling teenagers bumping into them to bring them back to the reality of Logan airport.

For Laura the interruption was a jarring reminder that if she didn't get moving, she was going to miss her flight.

Sam spoke her thoughts aloud. "I guess you better go get on that plane before it takes off without you."

"I guess I'd better." But she made no move to leave. She didn't want to go.

"Come here, you." He tugged her into his arms.

Necessity dictated that the kiss be brief, but what it lacked in duration it made up for in intensity. His mouth slanted across hers until he wasn't simply kissing her; he was possessing her, just as she'd taken possession of him.

In the end Sam was the one who had to be strong. He broke off the heated embrace, setting her away from him with hands that shook slightly.

"I said it once, and I'll say it again," he muttered huskily. "You pack quite a wallop, lady."

Laura smiled. "So do you, Sam. So do you."

Then there was only time for one last hug before she had to hurry through security.

Sam started missing her before she was even out of sight. The loneliness intensified as he watched her disappear into the crowd. By the time he'd waited around to make sure the flight had gotten off safely, he was downright depressed.

Turning on his heel, he headed for the nearest airline ticket desk. "I need to buy a ticket to Toronto," he announced curtly. "Got anything for this afternoon or tonight?"

"No, I'm sorry," the ticket agent replied, looking down at his computer terminal. "Those flights are all sold out. We do have seats available on the morning flight, though."

"Fine." Sam slapped down his credit card. "I'll take it."

"I can do this," Laura muttered to herself as she stood looking out the window in her hotel room. "Think positively. I *can* do this! It's just a speech." She tried focusing her attention on the lovely view of Lake Ontario. Wouldn't it be nice to be out there on the lake, with the wind in her face, enjoying a ride on a sailboat? Or walking along the wharf and looking at all the goodies in the store windows? To relax and forget all about...

"Forget?" she repeated, her heart suddenly lodged in her throat. "Oh, no! I didn't forget my notes, did I?" Winging it in front of a crowd of one hundred people was not her idea of a good time.

Racing for her as yet unpacked luggage, Laura wasn't satisfied until she'd retrieved all three copies of her presentation: one from her purse, one from her briefcase and one from her suitcase. She sighed in relief. "Okay. It's okay. They're all present and accounted for. Calm down. Relax."

Her one-way conversation continued as she finished unpacking, turned the TV off and on, picked at the salad she'd ordered from room service and then took a hot bath. She thought she'd succeeded in relaxing a bit but realized that wasn't true when she jumped at the sound of the phone ringing.

It was Sam. "So you got there all right, huh?" he said.

"Yes. The hotel is lovely, right on the lake. I can even see a bit of the skyline from my window. The room's nice, too."

"And how's the conference going?"

"It doesn't actually start until tomorrow morning. I'm already nervous. About my speech and everything."

"Don't worry about it. You're a pro at this."

She grimaced. "Sure."

"I've got something in mind that will make you feel better."

"Oh? What's that?" she asked.

"I can't tell you. You'll find out soon enough."

"This sounds mysterious."

"Mysterious is my middle name."

"Sam Mysterious Mitchell? I don't know," she mused. "I suppose it has a certain charm to it. Just like its owner."

"Sure," he retorted. "*Now* she flatters me. Now that she's not even in the country. Let's see how daring you are next time we're face-to-face."

"Is that a challenge?"

"You bet it is."

"Fine. You're on."

"I know," he said in a sexy drawl. "And you're the one who made me that way."

"Sam!"

"What?" When she made no reply, he said, "I'll bet you're blushing, aren't you."

"Of course not."

"I think you are. And I wish I was there to see it. Tell me," he lowered his voice to a sexy undertone, "what are you wearing right now?"

Two can play at this game, she thought to herself with a grin. Settling back against the pillows, she stalled for time. "What am I wearing right now? You mean, right this minute?"

"Right this second."

"Nothing." Hearing his startled exclamation, she couldn't resist teasing him. "Now I'll bet *you're* blushing."

He groaned. "Don't you know it's dangerous to taunt a man over the phone like this? You almost gave me heart failure."

"Would you feel better if I told you I was wearing a flannel nightie that goes down to my ankles?"

"You're not really wearing flannel, are you?"

"You don't want to know what I'm *really* wearing."

"Yes, I do. Trust me. I do."

"You remember that blue nightie?" she murmured softly. "The one from Lilly's window?"

He groaned again.

She grinned. "Well, I'm *not* wearing that."

"Shame on you, you wicked, wicked woman—torturing me this way."

She laughed. "After all this, you're going to be disappointed with the truth."

"I doubt that."

She laughed again, a little more self-consciously this time. "I'm just wearing a pair of pajamas."

"And filling them out quite nicely, I'm sure."

She cast a doubtful look down at her shirtfront. "I don't know about that."

"I do," he stated confidently.

"You're telling me you're an expert on how women fill out a pair of pajamas? I don't know that that's exactly something to brag about, Sam."

"Are you jealous?"

"Should I be?" she countered.

"No."

"Then I'm not."

"Good."

They talked a while longer. When Laura looked at the time, she was startled to see that almost an hour had gone by.

"Listen, this call must be costing you a fortune," she said.

"I can afford it," Sam retorted. "I'm not exactly a pauper, you know."

"I didn't mean—"

He cut her off. "I know what you meant. And you're probably right. No sense giving all my money to Ma Bell when I could be spending it on better things. Things like that little blue number from Lilly's. See you soon."

"Good night, Sam," she said softly. "Thanks for calling. I really appreciate it."

"No problem." As Sam hung up the phone, he hoped there wouldn't be any problems with his surprise the next morning.

To his delight he found her right away. She was in the hotel lobby. And she was surprised, all right. She looked downright shocked.

"Sam! What are you doing here? You're supposed to be in Boston."

"I decided to surprise you," he said.

Not now! Don't surprise me now! she frantically thought to herself. Neither she nor her stomach could take any more surprises. She'd already gone through half a roll of antacids. She'd had so little sleep she was surprised she was even halfway coherent. Whether or not she'd be able to stay upright for her speech remained to be seen.

"Dr. Peters, your presentation begins in five minutes," her moderator warned her. "We'd better get going."

"Sam, I'm sorry." She rubbed her fingers together in nervous agitation and then jammed them into her pockets. "I can't talk now. I've got to go give my speech."

"Want me to sit in and listen?" Sam inquired.

"No!" She could tell by the look on his face that her refusal had upset him, that he was thinking she was still ashamed of him. But a crowded hotel lobby wasn't the place for her to correct his misinterpretation of the situation. "Sam . . ." The way she spoke his name pleaded for his understanding.

"You'd better go," he said curtly. "You've got a speech to give."

"Will you still be here when I'm through?"

"Maybe."

"Dr. Peters!" Her moderator gave an impatient look at his watch.

"I'm coming." Turning to face Sam, she removed her room key from her pocket and discreetly pressed it into his hand. "Please wait for me," she requested softly. "We'll talk then, Sam. I promise."

"That's not all we're gonna do, lady," Sam muttered as he watched her walk away from him yet again.

Seven

Laura dabbed a cold, wet paper towel against her forehead as she stood in the women's washroom. She'd finished her speech a short while before without making too large a fool of herself and had headed straight here. It was ironic that the topic of her speech had been "Anxiety Control in Pedodontia Patients" when here she was recovering from an anxiety attack.

A few deep-breathing exercises, a little more cold water on her face, and she was ready to face the world again. She was even able to smile at several of her colleagues as she waited for the elevator to rescue her, whisking her from the hotel's congested conference level to the privacy of her room—and, she hoped, the welcoming arms of an understanding Sam.

The elevator did its part, but as soon as Laura walked into her room, she knew Sam wasn't going to do his. He wasn't in an understanding mood. One look at his stormy face, and her stomach quivered at the prospect of more stress.

"You're angry," she noted warily.

"Damn right I am!"

"Why?"

"Why? I can't believe you're even asking me that question! Why? Because I came all this way to see you and you brushed me off as if I were trying to panhandle you for money."

"You're exaggerating a little. Okay, so I wasn't as welcoming as I should have been perhaps, but I was surprised to see you. And aside from that, you happened to have caught me at a very bad time."

"Caught you at a bad time, huh? Fine. I can fix that right now." He grabbed his overnight bag. "I'll just leave."

"Sam!" She grabbed his bag, too, and the two of them engaged in a tug-of-war. "I'm getting a little tired of you storming out whenever you don't like something."

"And I'm getting a little tired of feeling like a second-class citizen around you," he shot back angrily. "First you want to keep our relationship quiet in Baileys Crossing, and now you act like I've invaded sacred ground by barging in on your conference. You didn't like me breaking up your little get-together with your other dental types. I don't fit in here. I don't belong here."

"Listen, there are times when I'm not sure I belong here, either," she admitted wryly. "Can we at least sit down and talk about this instead of standing here wrestling over your bag?"

He made no verbal agreement, but to her relief he did set his bag down and sat on a corner of the bed—the corner closest to the exit.

"If you'd told me you were coming, I would have reacted differently," she said. "As it was, I was a nervous wreck. I always am right before I have to give a talk. I told you that."

Sam knew she'd said that, but he hadn't really believed it at the time and he didn't believe it now. "What have you got to be nervous about? Getting on a plane when you're afraid of flying, now *that's* something to get nervous about."

"You're afraid to fly?"

"Let's just say I'm not real comfortable with it," he muttered.

"Then why did you come after me?"

"Believe me, I've asked myself that question several times while I sat here waiting for you to come back. I came because I missed you and mistakenly thought you'd be glad to see me. Boy, was I wrong."

"You weren't wrong."

"*You* weren't glad to see me," he retorted.

"I was surprised."

"I saw the look on your face. It wasn't surprise as much as horror. It's not a look I want to see on your face again— the classy lady dentist upset by her renegade boyfriend showing up where he's not wanted."

"You are wanted."

"Sure I am. Just not where anyone in Baileys Crossing can see us. And not where any of your professional colleagues can see us, either. Well, that won't wash anymore. You claim you're not ashamed of me, but I think your actions speak for themselves."

"So, we're back to this again, are we?" She sighed and sat down next to him. Their shoulders touched. "I guess it's time I filled you in a little more about my background." She took a deep breath before proceeding. "You know how you're always referring to how classy I am? It's all an act, Sam. I didn't grow up the way you think I did."

"And what way is that?"

"With a silver spoon in my mouth. Far from it. In fact, when I was growing up we had dented secondhand spoons my aunt picked up from the Salvation Army store down the street. To put it bluntly, we were poor. Not quite destitute—we never slept outdoors or went without a roof over our heads. But there were plenty of times when we'd go without electricity, and sometimes without heat, because there wasn't enough money that month to pay for it. Your standard of living while you were growing up was actually much, much higher than mine was."

Sam was surprised. "You were poor?"

She nodded. "Dirt-poor."

"Why didn't you tell me any of this before? Are you ashamed of where you come from?"

"It's not a matter of being ashamed. It's hard to tell people about my background without them feeling sorry for me or without it sounding as if I'm wallowing in self-pity."

"It might be hard to tell *people*, but I'm not people. Did you think the fact that you grew up poor would make any difference to me?"

"It makes a difference to me. In ways I can't explain. It's part of what's made me the person I am today."

"And what kind of person is that?"

"Someone who's very different on the inside from the way I look on the outside. You once told me that when you looked at me you saw a self-confident superwoman who's got it all—a town house, fancy car, flourishing dental practice..."

"Yeah." Sam was clearly waiting for the punch line.

"Well, that's not me."

"What do you mean it's not you? You've got a dentistry degree, you've got a town house, you've got a BMW."

"Forget the degrees, forget the trappings. I'm talking about the real me. In here." She pointed to her heart. "In here I'm desperately afraid someone is going to find out that

I'm not as smart or as classy as I pretend to be. What kind of person does that make me?'' She gave him a wry smile. "A mixed-up one, I guess,'' she concluded.

"Mixed-up, you say?'' Sam looked at her a moment, his gaze filled with affection and acceptance. "Personally speaking, that's always been my favorite kind of person. Must have been what first attracted me to you. That and your great legs, of course.''

"They're not that great,'' she murmured self-consciously, crossing her ankles and tugging the hem of her skirt down.

"Trust me. I know legs. They're great. Why does being great at something make you feel so uncomfortable?''

She shrugged. "Living up to high expectations sometimes means you're always reaching and never achieving. Do you remember saying once that I must have been the brains in my family?''

Sam nodded. "And I remember you weren't real pleased about me saying that.''

"It hit a sore spot with me,'' she admitted. "When I was growing up, my cousin was the sensitive one and I was the smart one—the one expected to know all the answers. I never even felt like I understood half the questions, let alone the answers. I was expected to use my brains to get me out of that poverty.''

"And you did get out. That's quite an accomplishment.''

"It's an accomplishment that anyone with a bit of drive and determination could have managed. My mom was the one who made all the sacrifices. When my father died, we had to move in with my mom's sister in order for my mom to go out to work. She didn't have any kind of training, so she had to take what jobs she could. She ended up working as a cashier in a supermarket, making minimum wage. She wanted things to be better for me.''

"And they have been better.''

"Yes, they have. So much better, in fact, that part of me is afraid that something might happen to take it all away."

"What could happen?" he questioned.

She shrugged. "I don't know. I could make a mistake." Uneasy at the thought, she slid her hands into her jacket pockets. "You know, I always thought successful people would feel differently inside. That they'd feel as successful as they looked. Maybe that's why I don't consider myself to be successful yet. Because I don't feel that way inside yet. Inside I still feel like I did as a child."

"And how's that?"

"Scared," she replied softly. "Scared that I won't measure up to other people's expectations."

"Why are you so worried about what other people think of you?"

"I'm not worried," she denied immediately. Seeing the look on his face, she sighed and admitted, "Okay, maybe I do worry just a tiny bit. Another character flaw of mine to add to the growing list. Chalk it up to the need to be accepted. Growing up the way we did, April and I... Well, let's just say there were plenty of times we felt like real outcasts from society. I can tell you one thing, though—certain people's opinions definitely matter more to me than others."

"Whose?" he asked.

She turned to look at him. "Yours."

"Then there's no problem. Because my opinion of you isn't likely to change. When I first met you...when you first knocked me off my feet, I thought you were classy. I still think you're classy. And okay, so I was wrong about the way I pictured your background. But that doesn't change the way I see you now. I saw the classiness in you first and created your background to match it. The classiness is in here." He gently touched her heart. "You just need to convince yourself of that in here." He moved his finger to her temple. "Because the problem may not be in how other people see you, but in how you see yourself."

"How'd you get to be so smart?" she whispered unsteadily.

"Maybe I know a thing or two about being labeled. About living up to other people's expectations, especially when they don't match your own." He grinned in a way that had become endearingly familiar to her. "Then again, maybe I'm just naturally brilliant."

"Maybe you are," she had to agree. "I'm glad you don't think I'm a complete idiot."

"Hey, I happen to love total idiots. One in particular. You."

Her breath caught in her throat. She looked at him uncertainly. "You're kidding, right?"

"Am I?" He brushed his lips across hers, and words were lost.

The kiss started out slow and sweet. His mouth explored the soft curves of hers—demanding nothing, and in doing so, receiving everything. Laura closed her eyes and opened her lips, giving him the invitation he was waiting for. Still he teased her a bit longer until she took up the pursuit, seducing him with her tongue.

She didn't even realize they'd drifted down onto the bed until she felt the mattress beneath her back. Even then, it didn't really register, distracted as she was by his lips. Sam wasn't just kissing her—he was making her his, tying her to him with gossamer bonds of want and need and . . . love. . . .

She'd been falling in love with him for some time. Loving him now seemed the most natural thing on earth, the only thing on earth at the moment. She wanted to share everything with him.

So she shared her delight with his kisses by returning them. She shared her appreciation of his warm body by tugging him closer. Then she shared her thoughts, murmuring her pleasure as he softly kissed her from her jaw to her temple.

He nibbled on her ear before whispering, "Nice jacket. Let's get rid of it."

He'd already unbuttoned it. With little effort, she slid it off.

He immediately set to work on another set of buttons. "The blouse is next."

She stilled his fingers. "What exactly are you trying to do?"

"Undress you. Now are you going to help or not?"

"Of course." She lowered her lashes demurely and undid the final two buttons. "I was just waiting to be asked."

"Well, forget waiting." He slowly parted her blouse to reveal her pale skin. He bent his head and kissed her there. "The waiting is over."

"I just have one more question. Why am I the only one being undressed?"

"I don't know." He propped himself up on one elbow. "You must be getting derelict in your duties. Better hurry up."

"Hurry up? I'll show you hurry up." In no time at all she'd tugged his shirt from his jeans, unbuttoned its buttons and peeled it off him. "Is that better?" she inquired with a grin.

Leaning on his side, he gently pulled her against his bare chest. "I don't know. You tell me."

"Mmm." She rubbed against him. "Much better."

"You sure you haven't been seducing men forever? 'Cause I gotta tell you, for an amateur you're incredibly good at this."

"Thank you, kind sir." Her fingers, which had been exploring the contours of his chest, suddenly ran into something other than warm flesh. "What's this?" She held up a medallion hanging on a chain around his neck.

"A Saint Christopher medal. I figured I could use all the luck I could get."

She let the medal swing back into place and then kissed his bare skin. "How brave of you to fly all the way out here to see me, despite your fear."

"It's not fear. It's discomfort."

"The same way you feel discomfort going to a dental office?"

"No. *That's* fear."

"You're not alone, you know," she told him earnestly. "I attended a workshop this morning where they said that an estimated twelve million people suffer from dental phobia, and that's just in America."

"Laura," he said with exasperation, "this isn't really the time to discuss statistics."

"I know. I'm sorry. I'm babbling. I guess I'm a little bit nervous," she finally admitted.

"There's no reason to be nervous."

She smiled at him. "That's what I tell my patients."

"This will be more fun than a visit to the dentist," he promised her.

"It hasn't been that much fun in the past." The admission was out before she could stop it.

"No? We'll have to change that." He seductively licked her lower lip, which moments before she'd been biting nervously.

At first his touch was soothing, coaxing, tantalizing. Then it was coaxing and tantalizing. Then it was plain tantalizing as he directed his attention to the pearly gates of her teeth, running his tongue over their smoothness with warm appreciation. Soon afterward his tongue engaged hers in a languid exchange that further fanned the flames. She was burning up, lost in the sensual pleasure.

"Has kissing ever been this much fun in the past?" he murmured, barely lifting his lips from hers.

"No."

Now his hands joined in the seduction, moving over her body with a gentle caress here, a heated stroke there. Exciting one spot only to move on to another. "What about touching?"

"No. It's never felt like this," she gasped.

"Then I don't think what happened in the past matters, do you?"

"No."

"This is here and now. Just you and me. And we've got all night." Providing I don't go completely berserk before then, he thought to himself with an inward grimace. The intensity of her response had him so wound up he was going to have to start reciting the multiplication tables, backward. But he'd do it, and whatever else it took to make this right for her. "We can take it real slow."

"We won't need all night," she told him with a sultry laugh.

"We won't?"

"No. And we don't have to take it that slow. You've already got me half-crazy. I think it only fair that I return the favor."

And she did, surprising him with her ingenuity and delighting him with her enthusiasm.

"All right," he gasped, rolling her onto her back. "Now you've done it! Now we're both crazy!"

Their tussle ended with her bra going the way of her blouse and jacket—into a pile on the floor. Laura had no cause for complaint, however, since instead of being covered by silk and lace she was now being covered by the gentlest, sexiest hands she'd ever imagined.

She forgot to be worried about her lack of cleavage. She forgot everything except for the way he made her feel.

He slid his hands down, over the skirt she still wore, beneath it to the garter he was sure he'd find there. "You know," he murmured as he released first one garter and then the other, "I've been dreaming about this moment ever since I found you fixing this at the warehouse."

"You caught me by surprise that day." She watched him, trying to hide her excitement at the sight of his big strong hands gently rolling her stockings down her legs. "You've done that a lot since I met you."

"The feeling is mutual," he admitted huskily.

She hoped it was. She hoped the love was mutual. She hoped for so many things, and he was making most of them come true—with just the temptation of his touch.

Her eyelids drifted shut, and her body opened up, blossoming with growing need. He was discovering her innermost secrets—what she liked, what gave her the greatest pleasure—and then acting on those discoveries in a way that left her breathless. Each time she came sliding down from the pinnacle of pleasure, he lifted her higher again.

She clung to him, trying to hang on to her reason. It was useless. The mindless ecstasy shattered her, washing over her in ever-increasing waves of surging pleasure. She sank back onto the pillow, feeling as if every bone in her body had simply melted away.

Laura vaguely heard the snap of Sam's jeans, the whoosh of clothes sliding over skin and the crinkle of the foil packet he'd removed from his pocket. All these sounds registered in some distant part of her mind. The rest of her was too preoccupied with the heavy pleasure seeping through her.

Surely she'd experienced it all now. What else could be left? A great deal, she soon found out to her delight.

He came to her slowly, carefully, making sure she was ready for him. She was. She accepted him eagerly, welcoming him, absorbing him into her very being. With every thrust of his body she became aware of a new anticipation, of a hunger that could not be denied.

Spiraling upward, Laura felt the need increase as the tempo changed. Slow and heated became fast and furious. Each rhythmic thrust of his hard body brought him deeper and deeper, and brought her closer and closer...

She gasped his name as suddenly it was all there, pulling her into its undulating vortex. What had begun as a tensing ripple exploded into surges of unadulterated ecstasy.

Sam shared in all the stages of her imminent climax—the heated softening, the silken tightening, the rippling convulsions that were now traveling from her body to his, snapping his control and triggering his own release. He groaned her name as he stiffened and then collapsed in her arms, knowing there was no place he'd rather be.

Eight

―――

Laura woke up with a start. Sam's arm lay heavily across her waist.

She smiled and looked down at his fingers, which were resting temptingly close to the curve of her bare breast. Then she looked at her travel alarm on the bedside table. Her smile disappeared. She couldn't believe it was so late! The day's barrage of workshops was scheduled to begin in an hour. Only now did it occur to her that she'd forgotten to set the alarm last night, or to request a wake-up call.

Of course there was a very good reason for her forgetfulness. Last night had been incredible. Thinking about it now made her feel all warm and tingling inside. But there had been more to the night than their lovemaking. There had also been moments when they'd just held each other and talked or been silent as the mood had hit them. The cuddling. The sharing. The laughter and the tenderness.

Her eyes reluctantly returned to the alarm clock. Fifty five minutes to the first workshop. Not much time for her to get ready.

Her thoughts returned to Sam. She hated to wake him. Taking a peek at him over her shoulder, she decided she could be late for the first workshop. He looked like a little boy—with his dark hair tousled and his nose stuck in the pillow. She turned toward him.

"Don't wake me," he murmured, tightening his arm around her waist and pulling her closer to him. "I think I've died and gone to heaven."

"I'm sorry. I didn't mean to disturb you." She patted his arm repentantly. "Go back to sleep."

"Where do you think you're going?" he demanded as she slipped out of his embrace and got out of bed.

"To the conference." She grabbed for a nearby robe and quickly tugged it on. "The workshops begin at nine."

He caught her hand before she'd taken more than two steps. "I thought you gave your speech yesterday."

"I did."

He brushed his thumb across the inside of her wrist. "Then why do you have to go to workshops today?"

"To learn about new dental techniques." Her answer may have been brisk, but her voice was anything but.

"I can teach you all about new techniques," he promised her in a darkly seductive voice. "Stay here instead and let me show you."

She let him do a lot more than show her. And he returned the favor, letting her practice her newly learned techniques on him to her heart's content.

And her heart *was* content, blissfully so.

"So, now that you've convinced me to play hooky, where will we go today?" Laura asked as the time on her alarm clock reflected the fact that morning was edging into afternoon.

Sam stretched like a contented lion before placing his clasped hands behind his head. "You mean you want to leave this room and this bed?"

"Well, we have been here for over fifteen hours now. Not that I'm complaining, mind. I just wondered what we were going to do today?"

He gave her a meaningful look.

"Aside from that," she said.

He grinned. "You're the one playing hooky. You choose."

"How about doing some sight-seeing?" she suggested hopefully. "Even though this is my second trip to Toronto, I still haven't seen anything aside from the airport and my hotel."

"What do you mean you haven't seen anything?" he demanded, highly affronted. "What about that time I turned the lights on when we were—"

She quickly clapped a hand over his mouth. "Toronto, Sam. I'm talking about Toronto and going sight-seeing. Does that interest you?" She removed her hand so that he could reply.

"Depends on the sights. The ones I'm looking at right now can't be beat," he murmured, eyeing the curve of her breasts where the sheet was just about ready to slide to her waist.

She tugged the sheet back into place with a demure smile that he couldn't resist kissing from her lips. Then he pulled the sheet away from her. "Well? What are you sitting there for?" he demanded. "Up and at 'em, girl! We've got places to go, things to see."

She yanked the sheet away from him, leaving him as exposed as she was. "There certainly are some wonderful, positively magnificent things to see!'' she agreed with a saucy smile. "You're absolutely right about that."

"I feel like a kid playing hooky from school," Laura said a short while later as they stepped outside into the early-June sunshine and she took a breath of the first fresh air she'd had since arriving at the hotel. "For a city, it doesn't smell too bad," she decided.

"That's because you're standing next to the flower beds." The roses were the same deep pink as her silk top. Sam had noticed that right away. That and the way the sun reflected in her hair, turning it to liquid gold. He knew she thought her white slacks and navy blazer were casual wear; she'd told him so. But she still looked crisp and classy to him. And beautiful. And a tad nervous. "What are you doing over there?" he asked. "Hiding so no one will see you?"

"Of course not."

"Then come on out here." He held his hand out to her and watched in amusement as she cautiously stepped forward. "That's better. You won't melt or be turned into stone for leaving a dental convention, you know."

"This is the first time I've done anything like this."

"Sure," he drawled, "that's what all the girls say."

She gently jabbed him in the ribs with her elbow.

"If you're through attacking me here in the street," he stated stoically, "maybe you'll tell me where we're supposed to be going so I can hail a cab."

"I thought we might go to Casa Loma," she said.

"What's that? A Mexican restaurant?" They'd ordered room service last night and this morning, but Sam supposed he could eat again.

"A restaurant? No, it's an honest-to-goodness castle complete with secret passages, towers and turrets," Laura replied. "At least that's what the tourist brochures say."

"Then let's go see if they're right."

The brochures hadn't lied, Sam decided as they got out of the taxi a short while later. Shading his eyes against the midday sun, he stared up in admiration at the masonry work of the promised turrets. "Yep," he noted. "It sure looks like a castle, all right. I'm impressed. What else does that brochure of yours say about this place?"

"Let's see..." Laura consulted the pamphlet in her hand. "That it was built from 1911 to 1914 at a cost of three and a half million dollars. Has ninety-eight rooms, not all of which are open to the public."

"Thank heavens." Sam was a fan of historical houses—how could he not be in his line of work? But even he couldn't face the prospect of going through ninety-eight rooms.

"Look," Laura pointed out, "they're about to start a tour. Do you want to join up?"

Sam nodded his agreement.

"If you'll all follow me," the guide said, "we'll begin our tour down in the wine cellar." Sam could have cared less about the wine cellar, but the details concerning the castle's foundation amazed him. "Forty-five feet deep?" he repeated, shaking his head. "They sure don't build 'em like that anymore."

As the tour continued up a secret staircase leading from the wine cellar to the study, Laura noticed that Sam was paying more attention to the structural facts and statistics than anyone else on the tour. It was the architectural salvager in him, she was sure.

He was intrigued by the weight of the conservatory's huge bronze doors, while she admired the delicate blues and greens of the stained glass dome overhead.

He was fascinated by the carved French oak paneling in the Napoleon Drawing Room, which the tour guide informed them took three craftsmen two years to complete. Even the mantelpieces on the fireplaces blew him away.

Laura was more interested in the people behind the possessions. The story of the castle's builder, Sir Henry Pellatt, seemed a fitting reminder of the fleetingness of wealth. Sir Henry had made his fortune and built the castle, only to lose them both in the end.

"Sir Henry was knighted in 1902 for being the first to bring electricity from nearby Niagara Falls," the tour guide went on. "Since he owned the power company, he'd had all the free electricity he could want and he equipped the castle accordingly. There were five thousand electric lights in the castle."

Laura stole a look at Sam to see if this, too, impressed him. It did. She smiled. She loved watching him. His face was so expressive. And the way his eyes crinkled at the corners when he smiled made her heart beat a little faster.

She only heard every third word the tour guide said after that. "...power company nationalized...Sir Henry hit hard times...couldn't even afford to pay the electric bills...back taxes...house contents auctioned off...lost his fortune...seventeen million dollars...only had thirty-five thousand left when he died."

It was a sad story—sad enough to temporarily take her attention away from Sam. Laura winced upon hearing how the hundreds of thousands of books from the library had been auctioned off for sixty cents each, regardless of their value. First editions, everything. Out.

As the tour proceeded to the second floor, Laura continued to gather impressions rather than statistics—the overwhelming size of the castle, the vastness of abandoned space. Such grandiose plans gone so awry. It felt like an empty movie set, so it came as no surprise to Laura to learn that Casa Loma had indeed been used as a location for several movies, including *Cocktail* with Tom Cruise.

How the mighty had fallen, she thought as they all tromped back downstairs.

"Taxes will do it to you every time," Sam noted. "You'd think the guy could have somehow scraped together the fifty thousand he owed. But then I guess fifty thousand dollars was a lot of money back in those days."

"It's a lot of money now," Laura replied. And she should know; the previous year she'd cosigned a loan with April for the restaurant for that amount of money. She'd been a bit nervous about it at first, but it seemed to be working out well. The last she'd heard, April and the restaurant were both holding their own.

Come to think of it, didn't she owe April a call? Or had April owed her one? Laura wasn't sure, but either way she'd have to give her cousin a call when she got home.

"Don't laugh, but this is the kind of place I imagined you growing up in," Sam admitted as they stood in the cavernous Great Hall at the end of their tour. "Well, maybe not quite *this* large . . ."

"Not even as large as *one* of these rooms. The four of us lived in a tiny one-bedroom apartment. My cousin and I slept in the Hide-a-bed in the living room. April still has that Hide-a-bed couch. She claims it's a collector's item now, since it was one of the first of its kind. I think she's just sentimentally attached to it."

"She has fonder memories of those days than you do?"

"She was younger. When the electricity went off, she thought it was a game. I thought we were all going to go to jail for nonpayment of bills. You know, debtor's prison, like you read about in Dickens."

Sam didn't want to tell her that he'd never read Dickens. He liked a good John le Carré or Tom Clancy thriller, though. And he was a sucker for Batman comic books.

"Anyway," Laura continued, "when I'd get scared and the lights would be out, either my mother or my aunt would come sit on the bed and tell us Ukrainian folk stories they'd heard from their mother. I can still remember my favorite one. It was about a mitten and all the forest animals, including a bear, that managed to squeeze into it one cold winter's day. My mom used to tell us that if all those animals could fit into that little mitten then we could certainly all fit in the apartment. It helped stop me from being so scared."

"When we were scared as kids," Sam said, "my brothers and I would tell each other scary ghost stories. The gorier the better."

"What did that accomplish?"

"We scared ourselves out of being scared. Frank, being the oldest and the smartest, would always come up with the best stories. Joey—the baby—would always end up crying and getting us all in trouble for being up so late."

"And you?" Laura asked. "What did you do?"

"Me? I was the one with the imagination. So I could usually picture Frank's monsters even better than he could."

"Didn't that scare you?"

"Naw. I'd just plan how to pay Frank back for making Joey cry. Used to come up with some pretty innovative ideas, if I do say so myself," Sam noted reflectively. "One time I put green food coloring up the water faucet in the bathroom. When Frank woke up in the morning and went to wash his face, his skin turned green. My folks weren't real amused, but I thought it was rather clever."

"It sounds like you were the practical joker in the family."

"Still am." It wasn't a role Sam relished any longer, but it was still expected of him. Others saw him as the happy-go-lucky one, but it wasn't how he saw himself. At least it wasn't the *only* way he saw himself.

"It doesn't sound like you're really pleased about being the practical joker," Laura noted.

"Let's just say that there are only so many times you can turn your brother's face green," Sam drawled, "without it growing old rather fast."

"Time to try red food coloring, hmm?" she suggested lightly.

"Yeah, something like that." He quickly changed the subject. "Listen, if you're up to it, there's another historical house next door. Want to check that one out while we're here?"

She could tell from the look on his face that he wanted to see it. "Sure."

Spadina was very different from its ostentatious neighbor. This house she loved because it was a home, a home that had obviously been well loved. From the freshly cut flowers in a vase by the front door, to the delicate Victorian watercolors on the walls, to the teddy bear in the upstairs nursery—there were special touches, lovingly placed and carefully attended, everywhere.

Spadina was almost fifty years older than Casa Loma, yet there was none of the feeling of abandonment here. Spadina had been lived in for several generations, and it showed. The feeling here was one of warmth and tender loving care. Laura noted the difference right away.

Sam, being the practical man that he was, was more interested in the original gaslight fixtures, which dated back to the turn of the century. Laura enjoyed seeing the kitchen, which looked like something right out of *Upstairs, Downstairs.*

In the end, Sam might have liked the billiard room best, but her favorite was the little area tucked upstairs—just beyond the staircase—called a "cozy corner." It was a place where family members would take a book on a sunny afternoon and curl up and read. Laura had such a space at the top of the stairs at her town house. She'd never known what to do with it. Now she did.

The gardens were as lovely and welcoming as the house, and even more colorful. Laura recognized the roses, iris, pansies, poppies and peonies. The names of the many other flowers were a mystery to her, but she enjoyed their beauty.

Sam was enjoying her beauty as she leaned down to smell one of the huge pink peonies. She looked so fresh, he suddenly wished he were the type of man who could come up with good compliments—the flowery kind, the kind that women liked. Better words than *great* or *beautiful*. Something poetic. Hell, he knew he was in deep when he started wishing he was poetic.

When he came close to her he found he couldn't resist putting his arms around her.

"I hope you weren't too bored tromping through stuffy old houses on such a beautiful day," Sam said, linking his fingers at the small of her back. "I should have warned you that I'm a sucker for these old places."

"I loved every minute of it." And she loved him. That thought drifted into her mind every time she looked at him.

"I'm glad," he murmured.

"Me, too."

He pulled her closer. "And what are you glad about?"

"That I'm standing here with you," she said softly. "What are you glad about?"

"The same thing."

They smiled and shared one of their "special looks." At least that's how Laura had begun labeling them. It was the kind of look that blocked everyone else out and locked the two of them in their own "cozy corner" of the world.

"So," she said, teasingly tugging on the belt loop at the waistband of his jeans, "what's next on the agenda?"

"A special romantic evening on the town," he announced. "I made reservations while you were in the shower this morning."

"Ah," she murmured. "A man who plans ahead. I like that."

"Ah," he replied. "A woman who admires a man who plans ahead. *I* like *that*."

That night, Laura wore the simple black dress she'd planned on wearing to the convention banquet and was instead wearing for her dinner with Sam. To jazz it up she added a red belt, red shoes and red beads—accessories that she'd originally brought to go along with a very business-like blue suit. They looked entirely different teamed with her basic black. This time her feeling of boldness matched the clothes she wore. She wouldn't be using her pockets tonight.

Sam was wearing his honest-to-goodness suit again, complete with a crisp white shirt and a blue tie.

He wouldn't tell her anything about the restaurant where they were going, advising her to be patient. "I think you'll like it" was all he'd say.

She did indeed like it. How could she not? After all, it was a Ukrainian restaurant. She was deeply touched by the gesture.

"How did you find this place?" she asked once they were seated.

"I looked in the phone book."

She smiled at his practical answer and picked up the menu. After a few minutes of studying the selections, she ordered chicken Kiev.

"I'll have that, too," Sam told the waiter, who nodded his approval of their choice before leaving them.

"They've got quite a crowd here tonight," Laura noted as she looked around. "It's a good thing you made reservations or we might not have gotten in."

"Mmm, I didn't expect it to be quite this crowded. Ukrainian food must be more popular than I thought."

"Maybe we should have been braver and tried the go-lubtsy, the stuffed cabbage," she said.

"Listen," he retorted, "I was being brave by not ordering plain steak or lobster."

"Yes, you were," she agreed with a smile. "I keep forgetting this is a new experience for you."

"It sure is. Getting dressed up in a suit and everything..." He tugged on his tie like a condemned man tugging on the rope around his neck.

"Poor baby," she crooned sympathetically.

With the arrival of their meal, conversation was temporarily put on hold as they both enjoyed the delicious food. The honey cakes they had for dessert reminded Laura of the cake her aunt had made for special holidays.

As they lingered over their coffee, Sam admitted, "You know, there are certain parts to this experience that I could get used to."

"Eating Ukrainian food, you mean?"

"Eating anything—with you."

"You say the nicest things."

"All the better to seduce you with, my dear."

"You've already seduced me," she reminded him with a sultry smile.

"You ain't seen nothin' yet."

"Oh, I wouldn't put it that way," she said demurely.

"What I meant was, there's seducing and then there's *seducing*," he explained.

"Really?" Her eyes widened in a deliberate show of astonishment as she placed her elbows on the table and leaned forward. "Tell me more. The mind boggles."

"The mind may boggle, but it's the body...the body that gets stroked and touched, kissed and licked."

"Licked?" she croaked, aroused by the ravishing roughness of his voice.

"Mmm, like this." He brought her hand to his mouth. When his tongue flicked the delicate web of skin between her thumb and her index finger, she was amazed at the pleasure that radiated through her.

"And here." Raising her wrist to his mouth, he used his tongue the way a magician uses his wand—to create magic. Black magic. The kind used to cast spells and charm maidens into surrendering. She was hooked.

"Where else?" she asked with breathless anticipation.

"Here." He ran his finger up to the inside crook of her elbow. "Here." He gently touched her throat, her collarbone. "And lots of other places we'll have to save for later."

Laura had to take a drink of ice water to cool down. She must have it bad, she noted absently. The lights were actually dimming.

"They must be starting the show," Sam said.

"What show?"

"I don't know. Whatever kind of show is traditional at a Ukrainian gathering. Violins maybe?" he suggested.

He wasn't even close.

The entertainment poured into the room with a vengeance. Cossack dancers in tall hats and outfits Sam wouldn't have been caught dead in. He had to give it to the guys, though. They sure knew how to kick up their heels.

"This isn't exactly what I had in mind when I was planning a quiet, romantic dinner," he muttered.

"What did you say?" she asked him, unable to hear him over the din of the entertainment.

"Nothing."

"This is great!"

"What?" he asked.

In order to hear her, Sam ended up moving his chair closer to her side of the table until he was sitting right beside her. As lively as the Cossack dancers were, he soon became distracted by the exotic smell of Laura's perfume. He leaned a bit closer, and couldn't resist kissing her. Meanwhile his hand slid under the table and found its way to her knee like a homing pigeon.

"What are you doing?" she whispered.

This time he could hear her since he was less than half an inch away from her. Sitting this close, he could practically read her lips. Or he could kiss them again. Just a light kiss, he told himself. Nothing heavy-handed. The heavy-handed stuff was going on under the table, as his hand slid up her leg to play with the garter he knew he'd find there.

"Sam!" She pressed her hand on top of his, trapping his exploring fingers between her dress and her upper thigh.

"What's wrong?" he asked with devilish innocence. "Aren't you enjoying the show?"

"I'm enjoying it a little too much."

"All right." He removed his hand and sat back in his seat. Way back.

"I didn't mean you had to move that far away," she said.

"No?"

"No."

He came closer again, this time entwining his hands with hers—above the table. "Better?"

"Safer," she replied.

But that feeling of safety didn't last long as their knees pressed together beneath the table. Each time she tapped her toe to the compulsive beat of the music, her leg brushed against his. Giving in to impulse, Laura slipped off one shoe and slid her nylon-clad toes against his leg. Sam retaliated by clamping his knees together and holding her captive. Their flirtation continued until they were both in such a state of excitement that they left before the floor show was over and headed back to the hotel.

The hotel room door had barely closed behind them before Sam was reaching for the zipper on her dress and Laura was reaching for the buttons on his shirt. She undid his tie with a skill she never knew she possessed. But then desperate times called for desperate measures. And she was desperate. For him.

Sam appeared to feel the same way. But he was better at removing clothes than she was. Faster, anyway. He had her dress in a pool around her ankles while she was tossing his tie over her shoulder.

"Mmm," he murmured, kissing the tip of her shoulder. "This looks familiar."

"I should hope so," she shot back with a grin. "It's my shoulder."

"I meant this." He fingered the strap of her white silk chemise and then smoothed his hand down to the matching tap pants. "This, or something damn close to it, was in Lilly's window that first day. And you said you never shopped there," he murmured with a reprimanding "tsk, tsk."

"Are you complaining?"

"Not me," he denied. "In fact, I brought you a surprise."

"I know and I can't wait to unwrap it," she whispered with a bewitching smile.

He stilled her fingers on the zipper to his slacks. When she looked at him uncertainly, he decided that he could give Laura her present—the infamous blue nightgown—later. Much later. There was no point having her get into a nightgown he was going to take right off her again.

"What?" she asked, confused by his behavior.

"Nothing." He swept her off her feet and carried her to bed. Then he returned her fingers to their original position. "I believe you were about to unwrap your present?" he prompted her.

She did—with a creativeness that left Sam breathless. Growling his approval, he rolled over so that she was perched atop him. Then he lifted the silk chemise over her head and tossed it onto the floor. Now her silk tap pants were the only thing that separated them. The brush of the smooth material against his arousal was like a piece of heaven and hell for Sam.

He tugged her down to him, kissing her lips with blatant hunger, thrusting his tongue into the warmth of her mouth the way he wanted to thrust his hard body into her womanly warmth. The rhythm was established, the pace hot and fast. He cupped her breasts in his fingers, awed by the way they fit into the palm of his hands. As he flicked his thumb over one rosy crest, he felt her shudder of pleasure and remembered his promise to stroke and touch, kiss and lick every inch of her body. His smile held the hard edge of anticipation. Sam Mitchell never made a promise he didn't keep.

At the first tantalizing lap of his tongue Laura was lost. When she arched her back with delight, her body brushed against his, and now Sam was the one who was lost. Reversing their positions, he discarded her silk tap pants with trembling fingers.

He traced a series of figure eights along her inner thigh, each time coming closer and closer to the one spot he had yet to touch—the one spot that ached for his touch. Then he was there—with one finger, two—teasing and tempting, brushing and stroking, driving her wilder and wilder. She rushed toward the peak, crying his name as ecstasy pulsed through her.

Laura's smile reflected her satisfaction. She felt wild and wicked. Bold and daring. So when he reached for the foil packet on the bedside table, her hand intercepted his. "Allow me," she whispered, taking the packet from his fingers.

She didn't falter once. His husky, heated words of encouragement made her feel powerful and desired. She held the evidence of just how much he desired her, caressing him as he'd caressed her. Then she guided him to her, sighing with delight as he surged upward, filling her with his throbbing warmth.

Now that they were intimately joined together, their lovemaking took on a slower, extended rhythm—a rhythm reflected in every heated stroke, every gliding thrust. Laura watched the expression on Sam's face. It was the first time he'd kept her eyes open, and now she knew what she'd been missing. He was watching her, too.

She tried to keep her eyes open, but when the tension built and the world came crashing in, her eyelids drifted shut while the fluttering ecstasy built to crescendo proportions. Her fingers dug into his back as she vaguely heard Sam shout his own release.

Much later, as they lay in the never-never land between satisfaction and slumber, they spoke in husky whispers about—of all things—the color of her eyes.

"They're really hazel, not brown," Laura maintained after he'd mentioned her big brown eyes.

"What's the difference?" he asked sleepily.

"They've got green in them."

"Where?" he demanded, squinting at her as he took a closer look.

"In my eyes. Mixed in there. Little flecks of green."

He moved closer until his nose was almost touching hers. "Oh, now I see them," he murmured. "Sure. Green flecks. Lots of 'em." Propping himself up on one elbow, he shook his head in amazement. "And to think all this time I thought I was falling for a brown-eyed blonde and now I find out she's really got hazel eyes."

"Disappointed?" She wasn't just referring to the color of her eyes, and Sam knew it.

"Not one bit. Intrigued. Fascinated. Hooked."

She hoped that was his way of saying he loved her. If that was the case, she'd use it, too. "Me, too."

She smiled and felt the effect her smile had on him. The tensing of his body beneath the sheets made her eyes open in surprise. "Are you . . . ?"

His smile was wolfish in return. "I am. Are you . . . ?"

She opened her arms. "I am."

Sam never did get around to showing Laura the night gown he'd gotten for her, but neither one of them minded.

Nine

"You're not nervous, are you?" Laura asked Sam as they took their seats on the plane heading back to Boston. Ever since they'd cleared American customs at Toronto's airport—a surprise for Sam, who'd wondered what American customs was doing in Canada—he'd been looking a bit peaked. To her eyes, anyway. And they were loving eyes that were learning to notice every detail about him.

"Nervous?" Sam repeated. "Why should I be nervous?"

"I thought you might be uncomfortable about the flight."

"Hold my hand and I'll feel better."

She immediately complied. "Sometimes it helps if you now what's going on," she told him. "Maybe if I talk you through the takeoff, you won't be as uncomfortable with it. That way you'll know what's coming. It works with patients who are afraid of the dentist. Sometimes it's the fear of the unknown more than anything else that bothers us."

Sam knew that it was Laura, rather than any fear of the unknown, that was responsible for him being "bothered," as she put it. She probably didn't even know she was responsible for the raging hormones seething through him. That was part of her charm, part of her sexiness.

It wasn't so much the way she looked, or even the way she acted, as the way she made him feel. It was an indefinable something that was as much a part of her as her classy walk and her hazel eyes—which Sam had decided were really brown. But, hey, if it made Laura happy to call them hazel, then he'd call them hazel. There wasn't much he wouldn't do for this lady. She didn't realize that yet, but he was beginning to.

It was an intimidating discovery for Sam that after years of playing at life, life had suddenly played back. With a vengeance. Here he was sitting in a plane, more afraid of what the future might hold than of the plane's takeoff, which Laura was so carefully trying to explain to him.

"Then the plane gets to the end of the runway and the pilot steps on the gas," Laura concluded, finishing up her lengthy and detailed accounting.

"Really?" Sam said, amused by her description. "Does he have a horn up there, too?"

"All right, maybe the technical term isn't stepping on the gas, but you know what I mean. Okay, we're almost through taxiing now. Sure you'll be all right? You aren't nervous?"

"No, but I might lose the feeling in that hand if you hold it any tighter."

"I'm trying to get your mind off the takeoff."

"I've got a few suggestions..." He leaned closer and whispered in her ear.

Neither of them noticed the plane taking off. It wasn't until the captain came over the public-address system and announced that he was turning off the seat belt sign that Laura became aware of what was going on. The devilish eam in Sam's eyes didn't reflect one iota of concern, let one fear.

"You big phony!" she exclaimed, releasing his hand and cking his arm.

"What'd I do?" Sam asked, grabbing her hand and re-ining hold of it.

"Said you were afraid to fly."

"I said it made me uncomfortable," he corrected her. "I ate the way your ears pop."

"Chew gum. Sugarless gum."

"See. I knew you'd be able to help me. And now that e've solved that problem, there's another pressing need I ave that perhaps you could help me with, Dr. Peters."

After all the things he'd whispered in her ear, Laura knew l about his needs, pressing and otherwise. "In an air-lane filled with people? I doubt that."

"There are ways..."

"Forget it," she retorted. "For someone who's never own before, you've certainly adapted well."

"No more fear of flying. You must have cured me," he id.

"Same here."

"I didn't know you were afraid to fly."

"There's flying and then there's *flying*," she told him chly.

"Oh. You mean...you haven't done much of that be-re? Felt that before?"

"Never. Nothing ever like that before." Her voice was a nooth purr.

"Now she tells me," Sam muttered, rolling his eyes avenward. "Sure you don't want to do a little 'flying' w?"

"Oh, I want to. But not in a plane filled with people. The ly private place is the bathroom, and believe me, there's

hardly enough room in there for one person to turn around
They'd probably have to take us out on a stretcher.''

"Yeah, but we'd die happy."

"We can still die happy," she replied. "Somewhere else."

"Spoilsport."

She smiled and patted his hand. "You sweet-talker, you.

Their conversation was momentarily interrupted by th
arrival of the flight attendant asking if they wanted a drink
Once she and the drink cart had moved on, Laura spok
again. "We haven't talked about what we're going to d
when we get back home."

"I left my car at the airport, so we can drive straigh
back," Sam said.

"No, I meant what we're going to do about us. You an
me. I just wanted to know if you had any plans in mind."

Sam shifted uncomfortably. He had plenty of plans, bu
none that he was ready to tell her about. Not yet. "No
really."

"Oh." She hoped she didn't sound too disappointed.

"What about you?" he asked. "You got any plans?"

"Not really."

"There you go then."

"I only meant that it might be a little difficult repeat
ing...that is, arranging... It would be a lot easier if we live
in a bigger city," she concluded with a sigh.

"Worrying about your reputation?"

"I don't know." She turned to look at him. "Should
worry?"

"I don't think there's any danger of you becoming th
Scarlet Woman of Baileys Crossing."

"No? What if your mother comes after me with
shotgun?"

"I'll protect you. I've done a pretty good job of it so fa
haven't I?"

"An excellent job. Superb. Outstanding."

"Trying to sweet-talk me again, huh?" he said.

"When have I ever tried to sweet-talk you?"

"There was that rather heated phone call your first night Toronto," he reminded her.

"Aside from that."

"How about the time you talked me into helping you at e Easter egg hunt and ended up sticking me into a bunny it."

"I didn't stick you into that bunny suit. You got into it all yourself."

"You still owe me for that, you know," Sam declared.

"I do? I thought I'd repaid that debt last night."

"No, that was repaying the fact that I didn't make you eet my family. You still owe me for the bunny suit."

"When are you going to collect?" she inquired. It was her ay of asking when they'd be together again.

"Sometime when you least expect it. You could be in your fice, torturing some small child, when I'll burst in, grab u, throw you over my shoulder and carry you off to rav- h you."

She replied in the same lighthearted vein. "Of course, ere's always the chance that I might show up at your of- e sometime when *you* least expect it and ravish *you*."

"Really?" He sounded delighted with the idea.

"You never know." She smiled. "It could happen."

"So long as it doesn't happen while Mabel's around."

"Wait a minute. Do I detect a double standard here?" she manded with teasing indignation. "It's okay for you to eal me from my office in front of my staff, but it's not ay for me to do the same in front of your secretary?"

"Of course it's okay. In fact, it would be great. It's just at you'd probably have to get past Mabel first."

"Don't worry about that. I can be very creative when the uation calls for it," she assured him.

"Yeah, I've learned that about you," he said. "It wa quite a pleasant surprise."

"Only pleasant?"

"Exceptional. Outstanding."

"That's better," she murmured appreciatively. "Doe that mean you enjoyed your first trip outside of the coun try?"

Sam nodded. "I could get used to this."

Laura thought she could get used to it, too. Used to hav ing Sam around all the time, having him in her bed at night in her shower in the morning, in her life. She hoped he fel the same way about her. She thought he might. He'd made a few veiled references to his feelings for her, but he hadn' said anything definite.

But she wasn't about to let that ruin her time with Sam She wasn't going to analyze things to death. She was jus going to enjoy. When the time was right, he'd say the words and so would she. There was no hurry.

They didn't hurry as they drove back to Baileys Cross ing, either. Once they were outside of Boston, Sam took the slow route instead of using the turnpike. It was a chance for both of them to steal a little more time together as the passed through the countryside in the full bloom of early summer.

By the time they arrived in Baileys Crossing, the sun wa low in the sky and twilight wasn't far away. Laura was sur prised at the sense of homecoming she felt the moment the passed the Welcome to Baileys Crossing sign, the one tha listed the population as 2,347.

"You know, that sign is no longer accurate," Laura pointed out. "The population of Baileys Crossing has gone up by at least one member in the past few months. Frank Jr."

"And my younger brother's expecting another baby thi winter," Sam told her. "I guess the Mitchell brothers are

doing their share in keeping you supplied with little pa-
ients. *Two* of the brothers are, anyway,'' he tacked on.

"What about you? Do you plan on having children of
your own?" she asked.

"Someday. Yeah. What about you?"

"Someday. Yeah," she softly repeated.

"Two or three would be plenty," he stated.

"I agree."

Sam hoped she'd agree to have those children with him,
but he was getting ahead of himself. Just because she looked
at him as if she loved him, just because she'd made love with
him as if she loved him... Okay. Maybe it did mean she
loved him, but he wanted to make sure first.

"It feels nice to be back, doesn't it?" she said.

"I suppose." Although Sam had to admit he'd had a
wonderful time in Toronto and he wasn't looking forward
to the logistical problems of making love to her here in
town—in front of everyone's curious eyes, curious eyes like
those looking at him right now as they passed Ralph's
Hardware and Feed Store. Sam waved.

"Who was that?" Laura asked.

"Ralph."

"The famous Ralph with the rain-predicting bunions?"

"That's the one," Sam confirmed.

"I thought you'd made him up."

"Listen, there are enough real characters here in town that
don't have to make them up."

"Speaking of characters," Laura said, "Smitty did come
and apologize for missing his appearance as the Easter
bunny."

"The only kind of rabbits Smitty is likely to see are the
ones resembling the mythical Harvey that Jimmy Stewart
saw in that old movie."

"I loved that movie!" Laura declared enthusiastically.
"That and *It's a Wonderful Life* are two of my all-time fa-

vorites. In fact, when I first saw Baileys Crossing it reminded me of the small town in *Wonderful Life*."

"Yeah? Well, there are times when it's more like *Nightmare on Elm Street*," Sam grumbled as he pulled in front of her house—on Elm Street.

"Obviously our tastes in movies differ greatly."

"As long as our other tastes are the same, I wouldn't worry about it."

Laura wasn't worried about it. After Sam had carried her luggage inside and kissed her goodbye, she felt as if she didn't have a care in the world.

If she could only bottle what that man did to her, she'd be rich, Laura thought to herself with a grin. Rich enough to be able to repay all those student loans still hanging over her head.

She was smiling happily when the phone rang. It was April.

"I'm so glad to hear from you!" Laura said as she curled up on the couch, preparing herself for a nice long talk. "I've been thinking about you. How are you doing?"

"Not so good."

"What's wrong?" Laura asked sympathetically. "Is it that boyfriend of yours again?"

"No. I don't know how to tell you this."

"Just tell me."

"Laura, we're in trouble. The business, the restaurant, it isn't working."

Laura heaved a sigh of relief. She'd been afraid something had been dreadfully wrong. But it sounded as if April were just suffering from work overload. She knew how that felt. "Any new business has a few bugs to work out. Be patient."

"I've been patient. It's the bank that won't be patient. Not anymore. I went to the accountant today. He says I'm going to have to declare bankruptcy!'' April started to cry. "I'm ... so ... sorry...."

"I don't understand," Laura said in a shaken voice. "I thought things were going so well."

"They were. At first. But the past few months, business has dropped off. Times are hard around here, people aren't eating out as much as they used to."

"You never said anything."

"I know. I kept hoping things would get better. I'm sorry. I never meant to do this to you. When I asked you to co-sign that loan with me, I was positive I could make a go of it. I'm so sorry. Tell me it'll be okay. Oh, Laura, tell me it'll be okay."

The cry, a familiar one from their childhood, hit Laura hard. She responded to April's cry instinctively, the way a mother does when she hears her child crying. "Shh. It'll be okay. Don't cry, April. It'll be okay."

I don't have a clue how, though, Laura was thinking in desperation. The loan, the money—lost. There had to be a way to fix it. She simply had to think about it. Work it out. Yes, that was it. She'd have to come up with a way to fix this mess.

"What're we going to do?" April asked in a small voice.

"We'll work it out. Don't worry. Give me the name of your banker and I'll call him first thing in the morning."

April gave her the information but added the warning, "It won't do any good. The man just wants his money. He's not the sympathetic kind."

"Let me see what I can do."

"Thanks, Laura. I feel better just having talked to you. I knew I would. That's why I called you as soon as I got home from the accountant's office."

"You should have called me sooner—when you were first having problems."

"I didn't want to bother you. And I really did think I could handle it on my own. It isn't fair for me to always depend on you. I know you're busy with your own life. I wanted to show you that I could do something on my own. Wanting to be independent really backfired on me, though. Laura, how are we going to pay that much money back? Even if I sell everything, the restaurant has a two-year lease on it and the landlord won't let me out of it. I've already checked. There's not much left. The accountant projected that when everything was said and done, I'd still owe about forty thousand dollars. I don't have it, Laura. Do you?"

"I can get it." She wasn't sure how, but she'd get it. She had to. April wasn't the only one who owed the forty thousand. As cosigner on the loan, Laura was equally responsible. "Let me talk to the banker tomorrow. We should be able to work out some sort of repayment scheme."

"I knew you'd think of something," April said in relief.

"I'll call you tomorrow night," Laura promised.

She hung up the phone and started pacing around her living room, hands in her pockets. She should have kept closer track of April's business venture, she told herself. She should have called her more often, insisted on hearing how things were going. But she hadn't wanted to sound as if she were constantly checking up on April. She didn't want her cousin to think that she hadn't trusted her. She had. She did.

Laura knew that April was as upset about this as she was, if not more so. Which was why she couldn't let April know how precarious her own financial affairs were. Sure she had a town house, but the bank owned most of it. Her down payment had been a drop in the bucket. As for the BMW, it was leased. Her accountant had recommended that move. Her credit cards carried a heavy load, and those never-ending student loans from dental school ate up the rest of her income.

She had money in savings. She'd use that. But it wouldn't be enough. She'd have to talk to her accountant tomorrow. There had to be a way. She was making good money. There had to be a way. She just had to find it.

Sam called her at the office the next morning. "I thought we could go to the BC Café for a secret rendezvous, otherwise known as lunch. What do you say?" he asked.

"Sure," she said absently, wishing the accountant would call her back. But his secretary had said he wouldn't be back until after three.

"You could sound a little more excited," Sam noted.

"Sorry. I'm all out of excitement today."

"That's what happens when you go a day without seeing me," he replied.

"I guess so."

Sam noticed Laura's preoccupation during their lunch. He was right in the middle of telling her what he considered to be one of his funniest stories when he realized she wasn't listening to a word he was saying.

"Mmm," she murmured as he paused. "That's nice."

Just to prove his point, he said, "I'm thinking of going to the moon. Want to come along?"

"Mmm."

"Maybe you'd prefer Mars? Or Pluto?"

"Mmm."

He waved a hand in front of her eyes. "Hey, anybody home in there? You didn't hear a word I said."

"Sorry. It's been a rough day." In more ways than one. The phone call to the Detroit banker that morning hadn't gone well at all. The bottom line had been that he wanted the money, all of it, and if there was a problem, the bank would have to turn the account over to an attorney. Of course than she'd be responsible not only for the outstanding debt but also for the legal fees and any court costs.

She tried to wipe all thoughts of the disastrous call from her mind as she concentrated on Sam and the stories he was telling her about an old movie theater where he was doing salvage work. She tried not to let him see that she was upset. She thought she'd succeeded until right before they left.

"Hey, you sure you're all right?"

"Yes," she said automatically. "I'm fine."

Sam could understand her being distracted for a day or two, but after three days of that kind of behavior, he began to wonder what was wrong.

He tried asking her. "You okay?" *Fine*. That was the only answer he ever got. *She was fine*. He knew it wasn't the truth.

He tried the understanding and empathetic approach. "Something wrong? Something you want to talk about?" No.

Then he got angry and tried demanding that she talk to him. She'd kindly but firmly refused to say a thing.

Finally Sam did what any red-blooded American male would do. He want to another red-blooded American male—in this case, Jerry—for answers.

"Laura's going through a rough time right now," Sam said as the two men shared a cup of coffee at the BC Café. The get-together late Sunday morning had been Sam's idea. "I appreciate all the support you've given her."

"No problem," Jerry said. "Laura was there when I needed her."

Jerry didn't go into details, but Sam already knew that Jerry and his wife were working out their problems with a marriage counselor. Laura had told him that much before she'd clammed up. But he wasn't there to talk about Jerry's problems; it was Laura's problem that concerned Sam.

"It's hard to get her to accept help," Sam stated with man-to-man candor.

"That's true," Jerry agreed. "I offered to do what I could with her current situation, you know, but she wouldn't hear of it. Not that I would have been able to offer much help—what with the new equipment we've committed ourselves to buy."

Sam didn't see what equipment had to do with anything, but he nodded and gave Jerry what he hoped was a commiserating look. "Yeah, it's tough."

"I'm glad she's decided to talk to you about it," Jerry said. "I told her to, but you know how she can be."

"Yeah, I know how she can be."

"Anyway, have you come up with any ideas to help her?" Jerry asked.

"Not yet," Sam parried. "What about you?"

"Forty thousand dollars is a lot of money to raise. Laura told me she could get all but about ten thousand of it. The problem, as you know, is that the bank in Detroit is being sticky about it and demanding everything now. The entire amount. She's probably told you all this herself, right?"

Sam gritted his teeth and nodded. She hadn't told him a thing, but she should have. Anger, fierce and red-hot, flared deep within him. It was all he could do to sit still and listen to Jerry filling him in on things he should have known himself.

"Then you know that her BMW is leased so she doesn't have any collateral in that," Jerry said. "There's the town house, but again she hasn't had time to build much collateral there, either. From what I gather, her down payment was small.... Anyway, the bottom line is that she doesn't have much she can borrow against other than her interest in our partnership. And she's already done that in order to gather the rest of the money. She's talking about selling the town house, but I'm not sure that would be a good idea. You might be in a better position to advise her on that than I would, what with your family being tied to the construction business. For a while there she was even talking about selling her interest in the partnership, but I think I've talked her out of that. At least I hope I've talked her out of it.''

Jerry paused to take another sip of coffee, leaving Sam stewing as he waited for him to go on.

''Of course,'' Jerry continued, ''when Laura cosigned the loan for her cousin, she had no idea that something like this would happen. It's a tough break, her cousin declaring bankruptcy that way. I think she's kicking herself for not having anticipated this.''

The pieces were beginning to come together now. Laura had apparently cosigned a loan with her cousin and that cousin had now declared bankruptcy, leaving Laura holding the bag. ''How could she have anticipated this?''

''I don't know. You'd have to ask her that.''

''I intend to,'' Sam said grimly. ''Believe me, I intend to.''

Within ten minutes Sam was pounding on Laura's front door. ''Why didn't you tell me?'' he demanded as he strode into her living room, mad as hell.

''Tell you what?'' she asked in confusion. ''What's wrong with you?''

''It's not what's wrong with me,'' he retorted. ''It's what's wrong with you. Why didn't you tell me about your cousin's bankruptcy? About the loan? About any of it?''

''How did you find out?''

''That doesn't matter. Why didn't you tell me?''

''It's not your problem.''

Her answer only added fuel to his already burning anger. ''No, my problem seems to be that I'm hooked on a woman who won't tell me when she's in trouble! A woman who doesn't tell me the truth!''

''I didn't lie to you,'' she protested indignantly.

"You didn't tell me the truth, either. I knew something was wrong. I asked you time and time again. But would you say anything? No!" Sam was shouting now.

"There was no point in my telling you. There was nothing you could do." She was about to add, "It was my problem," when Sam interrupted her.

"How do you know there's nothing I could do? You never even bothered to find out. So what does that make me, huh? Good enough to sleep with, good enough to spend the weekend with, but not good enough to come to when there's trouble."

"It's not a matter of being good enough," she denied.

"No?" His expression was grim, any trace of his usual good humor erased. "Then what? You didn't think I was smart enough? Rich enough? It doesn't matter what adjective you use. The bottom line is that when you ran into trouble, you didn't run to me. You told Jerry what was going on, but you didn't tell me."

"I only told Jerry because I had to. I had to explain to him why I wouldn't be able to contribute toward the new rental equipment we'd planned on buying."

"Right." Sam's clipped voice reflected both his disgust and his disbelief. "You're real good at coming up with excuses."

"It's not an excuse—"

He ruthlessly cut off her denial. "I don't care. You still should have told me. You should have come to me. You're my woman. I can look after my own."

"What's with this 'my woman' stuff? Sam, we're not talking about protecting me from marauding Vikings here. There's not much you can do to protect me from a hard-headed banker who wants his money yesterday. You're in no position to help me."

His face hardened. "Right. There's nothing a small-town boy like me can do for a big-city fancy lady like you. Except in bed."

Laura flinched as if he'd struck her. "If that's the way you feel about it, then maybe you'd be better off without this big-city fancy lady in your life. I think you should leave."

"Fine. I'm outta here!" The slam of the front door marked his departure and left Laura with nothing but the memory of all the hurtful things they'd said to each other.

Ten

Laura simply stood there for the longest time—numbed by what had just occurred. Sam had walked out, yet again. Only this time she had a feeling it was for good.

She couldn't blame him. As she'd told him, he was better off without her. After all, what did she have to offer him? Nothing but her love and a financial debt that would take her years to repay.

Things had definitely not gone according to plan, she noted with semihysterical dismay. She'd hoped to turn this mess around and have it solved before telling Sam. But now it didn't look as if there were going to be a way of turning it around.

Laura didn't realize she was crying until she felt the wet, salty drops falling onto her clenched hands. And once the tears started, there didn't seem to be any way of stopping them.

There were so many things she could have told Sam. She could have told him about the many times she'd picked up a phone to call him, only to chicken out at the last minute. She could have admitted that there had been times when they'd spoken on the phone that she had planned on telling him, had wanted to tell him. Something had always held her back. Two somethings, actually. Fear and guilt.

The guilt—that had ties going way back to a promise she'd made to her mother and her aunt before they'd died. She'd promised she would look after April. And to her way of thinking—which didn't allow any E's for effort—she hadn't done a very good job of keeping that promise. Sure she'd cosigned the loan, but she hadn't done any follow-up work, and now she and April were both in financial hot water.

And the fear? That came from knowing that she'd screwed up, and knowing there wasn't much she could do to fix it. She'd spent hours with her accountant, juggling figures until she couldn't even think straight. The accountant told her there were ways she could have protected herself, things she should have done differently. She'd failed.

For her, failure brought with it a sense of unworthiness. She'd always feared that love was conditional. Maybe that's why she'd always tried so hard to avoid making mistakes, to avoid failure. She hadn't wanted to test the possibility that love could be taken away as easily as it was given. That's why she'd tried to hide her failure from Sam—for all the good it had done her. He'd found out about it anyway and the results had been just as disastrous as she'd feared.

She tried to wipe the tears from her eyes. She couldn't see straight anymore. Her vision was blurred, her mind overwhelmed. And the pain gnawed at her like a rabid animal.

When her pager beeped, Laura was so startled that she jumped. It took her a moment or two to piece things together. This was Sunday—her day to be on call at the office. The pager going off meant there was a dental emergency. She had to deal with it. And she did, by putting her own pain into a locked corner of her soul.

"It will be all right, Mrs. Mundi," she told the frantic mother a short while later. "Daryl chipped his front tooth when he fell off the bike, but he didn't crack it." Laura went on to reassure the anxious woman that her son would be fine, discussing the results of the dental X-rays with her.

All the while Laura wondered how much longer she'd be able to stay in Baileys Crossing, how many more little boys' chipped teeth she would be able to fix before the financial wolf at her door stopped knocking and just walked in. Her partnership was in jeopardy. If only...

But she couldn't think about any of that now. She had a patient to see to. Despite her earlier trauma, her hands were bedrock steady as she completed working on the accident-prone Daryl and gave him a badge for being such a courageous patient.

"I didn't cry once," Daryl bragged to his mother, and then turned to Laura for confirmation. "Did I, Dr. Peters?"

"You were very brave, Daryl. Although there's nothing wrong with crying every once in a while," she added.

"That's sissy stuff," the little boy stoutly maintained. "Batman would never cry."

Batman might not, but Laura certainly did her fair share of crying later that night. When she returned to the office Monday morning, it was with the hope that the Visine had gotten the red out of her bloodshot eyes. She'd never been a pretty crier. Now she just wanted to be a discreet one.

To give them credit, Sandy and Hazel both were on their best behavior, not asking her one personal question. Although they hadn't said anything, Laura knew that they were aware of her financial difficulties. With an office staff as small as theirs, it was difficult to keep secrets. Sam had once told her the same thing about small towns. No doubt he was right about that, too. She hoped he was doing better than she was.

By late afternoon Laura couldn't take the silence any longer. She decided to spill the beans to Hazel, who would in turn tell Sandy anyway. So when the last patient had gone for the day, Laura sat down with Hazel in the small room that served as a consulting conference room.

"All right, Hazel," she said rather wearily. "Just tell me how much you already know and that way I won't repeat myself."

"You blew it."

Having grown accustomed to the older woman's bluntness, Laura wasn't surprised by Hazel's words. "I know. I'm going to be in debt for the rest of my life."

"I'm talking about Sam," Hazel stated.

This time Laura was startled. "You are?" Word certainly had gotten around fast! She and Sam had only argued yesterday.

"Did you know that I got two phone calls from Mabel today demanding to know what you'd done to her boss to turn him from a great guy into Attila the Hun? He's yelling at everyone," Hazel stated.

"He'll get over it." She might not, but she had to believe he would.

"What makes you think that?" Hazel demanded.

"He thinks I just used him."

Hazel wasn't about to let things rest there. "What makes him think that?"

"The fact that I didn't tell him about the problems I've been having."

"Sam didn't know?"

Laura shook her head.

"Then I can see why he's mad."

"He's not just mad," Laura said. "He's furious. He claims I didn't tell him because I didn't think he was capable of helping me. That I think he's only good for—" Laura decided to rephrase his words "—a fun time."

Hazel nodded sagely. "I can understand why he'd react that way."

"You can? I sure couldn't. I never thought of Sam that way."

"Maybe you haven't, but others have. Sam's well liked because of his sense of humor. He's not exactly known for being the serious type."

"Maybe he'd like to be," Laura murmured. "Now that I think back on it, he didn't sound very pleased when he told me about being called the practical joker in the family. I should have picked up on it then. But I was so worried about my own labels that I never considered Sam might have some of his own to contend with."

"One thing is certain. Men don't appreciate being left in the dark," Hazel stated. "It makes them feel left out. They want to be taken seriously. When you didn't tell Sam about your problems, you weren't giving him the chance to help you, provide you with support, protect you—all those good things men want to do for the women they love."

The woman he loved? He'd called her "his woman," and he'd said he was hooked on her, but . . . "Sam has never actually said he loves me," Laura felt compelled to point out.

"Are you sure? Never? Not even in a way that made you think he was kidding?"

I happen to love total idiots. One in particular. You. She heard the words again, as clearly as if he'd just spoken them.

Reading the answer on Laura's face, Hazel nodded with satisfaction. "I thought so."

"I didn't realize he was serious. I mean... I hoped he was but . . ." Laura shook her head and jammed her hands into the pockets of her lab coat. "Oh, Hazel, it doesn't matter at this point," she declared dejectedly. "Sam's better off without me."

"Do you love him?"

Laura nodded.

"Then how can you not be good for him?" Hazel countered.

"Because all I seem to do is make him feel bad. And with this financial mess I'm in—"

"Sam's not interested in your money or lack thereof. I think you already know that."

"He deserves better," Laura maintained.

"Sounds like something Sam would say," Hazel retorted.

Laura's smile was bittersweet. "He did say that to me once."

"And was he right?"

"No."

"I rest my case." Hazel shook her head. "Young people today. I tell you. What's the world coming to when two people who love each other don't deserve each other? Don't be so hard on yourself. You deserve to be happy. Stop being the first to take the blame for anything that goes wrong and the last to accept praise when things go right."

"Do I do that?" Laura didn't realize she'd been so obvious.

"Yes. You do that. Stop it," Hazel admonished her with a gentle pat to Laura's arm. "And stop thinking Sam's better off without you. Because he's not. Now that's all the advice I'm going to offer you, although I'm dying to give you just a bit more...." Hazel visibly restrained herself. "No, that's all I'll say. I guess the rest is up to you. Think about it."

There was no place in Baileys Crossing that Laura could go and *not* think about Sam. A walk in the park conjured up memories of him dressed in the bunny costume. A visit

the BC Café brought back the fact that French apple pie
as his favorite. Even a walk down the street wasn't safe.
here was Ralph's Hardware and Feed Store, where Sam
ad waved at Ralph.

And then there was Lilly's. The next day, on her lunch
our, Laura needed to pick up some things from the drug-
ore. There was no way of getting there without passing
illy's. And when she saw Lilly herself out watering the red
etunias in her store's window box, Laura knew there wasn't
ny way she'd be able to hurry on by. Frustrated, she im-
ediately stuck her hands in her pockets.

"Dr. Peters!" Lilly greeted her. "So nice to see you. You
aven't stopped by lately. I know you must be busy. I just
anted to thank you again for the miracle you've worked on
y little granddaughter Jessie. She was so petrified of den-
sts before you came to town. She told me you sent her a
ard for her birthday. That was nice of you."

"Jessie's a sweet little girl. I'm glad I was able to help."

"You know Sam told me that you two met here in front
f my store. I thought it was so romantic." Leaning closer,
illy lowered her voice confidentially. "I believe he got you
little something special from my store last week. That blue
ightie that I had in the window. Mumbled something about
being for his sister-in-law, but I've known Sam since he
as knee-high to a grasshopper and I can tell you he didn't
et it for any sister-in-law. Since I know he's not the type to
e seeing two women at once, I knew it had to be for you.
h my gosh—" Lilly put her hand to her mouth in dismay
—I didn't ruin a surprise, did I? My husband always did
y that I speak first and think second. I hope I didn't ruin
nything."

Laura shook her head. "You didn't ruin anything." *I did
at all by myself.*

* * *

"You're the oldest. You go talk to him," Joey was saying to Frank as the two brothers stood in the relative safety of the warehouse's outer office.

Frank shook his head. "Forget it. I value my life. Why don't you talk to him?"

"Same reason," Joey answered.

"Well," Frank said, "somebody's gonna have to do it."

They both turned to look at Mabel, who shook her head. "Forget it, boys. Count me out."

"Come on, Mabel," Frank coaxed her. "You can do it. What's the worst thing he could do? Fire you? He's already done that three times today."

"Four times," Mabel corrected him, "and I'm not going in there. He's your brother. You talk to him."

"Maybe we should call the folks in on this one," Joey suggested.

Frank shook his head. "He'd just tell them to butt out, same as he told us."

"Well, somebody's got to do something."

Inside the office, the topic of their conversation was sitting back in his chair, feet propped on his desk. Sam was thinking about Laura. In particular he was remembering a conversation they'd had when he'd asked her what she liked best about being a dentist. "The smiles," she'd said.

Sam hadn't done any smiling since he'd walked away from her. He kept remembering what she'd said, about him being better off without her. He should have denied it, but hell, he'd been furious with her. Part of him still was, but most of him was plain torn up from the hurting.

Cursing softly, Sam rubbed at the knot in the back of his neck. God, she was stubborn. More stubborn even than this damn crick in his neck. That should teach him to fall asleep at his desk, the way he'd done last night.

He frowned at his surroundings. He never had gotten around to redoing the office. There still weren't any fancy plants anywhere, and the venetian blinds continued to hang as crookedly as ever. Sam had decided there was no sense fancying the place up, trying to make it look like something it wasn't.

He'd decided the same was true about himself. He wasn't fancy. He was a plain, straightforward, down-to-earth, somewhat old-fashioned guy who also happened to be a one-woman man. It was just his luck that his "one woman" was a brainy blonde who drove him up a wall with her convoluted thinking.

His gaze returned to the papers spread out on his desk, the papers that had kept him up most of the night. They held more doodles than numbers, but a plan was beginning to take shape in his mind. A plan to help Laura.

When the office door opened, Sam glared, ready to verbally jump on the person who'd dared to barge in and interrupt him. But no one came in. Instead, a white handkerchief tied onto the end of a yardstick was slowly being waved through the door's opening.

Then Frank, Joey and Mabel came into the room. "We've come to discuss peace terms," they announced en masse.

"I'm not in the mood for jokes," Sam growled.

"No kidding," Joey muttered.

"Yeah, we had noticed that," Frank added.

"So, what do you want?" Sam demanded.

"For you to start acting like a human being again," Frank stated.

"Look, we've figured some stuff out for ourselves," Joey said. "We heard about Dr. Peters's financial problems."

At Sam's glare, Frank reminded him, "Hey, it's a small town. Word gets around."

"Now," Joey continued, "we know you've gone off the deep end for this woman, so that leaves us with the knowledge that you wouldn't have dumped her in her hour of need. Which must mean she dumped you, right?''

Mabel jabbed Joey's ribs with her elbow. ''Oh, that was very sensitively put,'' she noted sarcastically.

''He's either gonna tell us or he's not, no matter how sensitively we put it to him, Mabel,'' Joey maintained.

''You might as well all sit down, this could take a while,'' Sam said.

''Does this mean you're going to tell us what happened?'' Joey asked.

''It means I'm gonna tell you what's *going* to happen. Listen up....''

Laura was tired. It was four in the morning, and she was standing in front of her freezer, eating Cherry Garcia ice cream straight from the carton. It wasn't working its usual magic on her.

Noticing the pile of papers on the dining room table, she headed in that direction. Since she was already up, she might as well get some work done. Sitting there, a spoon in one hand and a red pencil in the other, she reviewed the page she'd written for her monthly dental hygiene column in the local paper.

She read it aloud. ''One of the most serious dental problems we see in very young children is nursing-bottle mouth which occurs when a child uses a bottle of milk, formula or fruit juice as a pacifier at bedtime. These liquids can collect around the teeth and cause tooth decay. So if you must give your baby a bottle at night, fill it with plain water only. This way, your child won't be missing Sam...*Missing Sam?*'' Laura repeated, and then sighed. There it was, his name written bold as brass in the middle of her article. What's more, she didn't have the heart to cross him off with her red pencil.

Frustrated, she pushed the article aside. It was no good.
No matter what she was doing, Sam was with her every
moment of the day and night. She missed him more with
each passing second.

Was he really better off without her? That was the question.

"What do you think?" she asked the carton of rapidly
melting ice cream. "That I'm nuts to be having this conversation with a carton of ice cream, right? I should be having
it with Sam."

She ate another spoonful. So what was the bottom line
here? Did she think Sam didn't need her? Why? Because he
didn't show it? Who else knew that he wasn't always the
practical joker? Who else knew that he hated brussels
sprouts? Who else knew that he used humor as a shield?

As she sat there and tried to picture a future without Sam
in it, a certain knowledge slowly seeped into her soul. He
was definitely the man for her. But how could she be sure
she was the woman for him?

She loved him. That was a given and nothing particularly in her favor. What woman wouldn't love Sam? He was
a extremely lovable guy most of the time—when he wasn't
being impossible and bullheaded.

Maybe that was the secret. Maybe that's what she could
give him that no one else could. Acceptance. She accepted
him for the man he was—for *all* the men he was. That meant
seeing him as he really was—a man with a great sense of
humor, but a man who kept his deepest emotions to himself. A man stronger than any she'd ever met, yet still possessing vulnerabilities that caused him to flare up like a land
mine whenever she inadvertently tripped over one of those
sore points.

She didn't want to label him or confine him to a narrow
box marked Good Guy or Bad Guy, Funny Guy or Angry
Guy. She just wanted to love him.

As for whether or not he'd be better off without her, that question became moot because she didn't intend to let him find out. She planned on staying right there by his side. But first she had to find him.

Eleven

———

Finding Sam proved to be harder than Laura had anticipated. She tried calling him at home before he left for work. No answer. She tried calling him at the warehouse during the day. Mabel answered, and Laura couldn't get any information out of her. All Mabel had said was that yes, Sam was in town. Yes, she would give him her message. No, she didn't know when he'd be back in the office. Try again later.

Laura called every half hour for the rest of the morning. When she gave her free prenatal presentation at the nearby hospital, she even called him from there. The answer was always the same. *He's not in right now. Leave a message.*

Instead of taking a lunch break, Laura had an appointment with Mr. Cohen, the vice president at the Baileys Crossing Savings and Loan.

"Don't do anything drastic yet," he said when she brought up the possibility of selling her town house. "The deadline the bank in Detroit gave you is still a week away. Wait a few days.''

''Yes, but if I don't come up with the money by then—''

''Something will come up,'' Mr. Cohen said cheerfully. ''You'll see.''

Easy for him to say, Laura thought to herself crossly. His neck wasn't on the line.

When she got back to the office, there was a call from April.

''I'm working on the landlord to see if he won't let me out of the longer lease for the restaurant,'' April told her. ''He said if I could find someone to sublease it from me, he'd be willing to accept that arrangement. That would free up more money that I could apply to the loan.''

''That would be great. I hope it works out.''

''You know I'll pay you back. Every penny, Laura. We may both be collecting social security by then, but I will pay you back.''

''I know you will.''

After hanging up with April, Laura tried calling Sam again. No luck.

She fitted a space maintainer for a boy who'd knocked his tooth out in a fight, and then tried calling Sam. No luck.

She tried to count the teeth in the mouth of an eighteen-month-old biting baby, and tried calling Sam again. Still no luck.

By five o'clock Laura was getting frustrated, angry and desperate. ''Okay, Mabel,'' she said in what had to be her dozenth call of the day. ''Let me put it this way. Is Sam *ever* going to return my calls?''

''When the time is right, you'll hear from him, I'm sure.''

''Maybe I should come over there and wait for him—''

''No! Don't do that.''

''Why not?'' Laura asked.

"Because we got a business to run here and we can't have people sittin' around gettin' in the way."

"I've got a business to run, too," Laura retorted.

"Then go run it. And wait for Sam to get in touch with you."

"For how long?" Laura demanded in exasperation.

"Long as it takes," was Mabel's laconic reply.

Laura decided it was time to sic Hazel on Mabel. "Find out what's going on. Do whatever it takes."

Hazel came back a short while later with some news, but not much. "I'm quoting one of his brothers here—'Sam's busy with a project that requires that he be out of the office a lot and that he put in extra hours. I think you'll have better luck reaching him tomorrow.'"

"If I don't, I'm going to go camp on his doorstep," Laura threatened.

"I don't think that will be necessary," Hazel assured her. "I think you'll be hearing from Sam real soon."

"What if he doesn't want to hear from me?" Laura asked, worried. "I mean, maybe he doesn't want me bugging him anymore."

"Then he'd tell you so himself. He wouldn't avoid you. Sam's not the type to do that."

"Mabel hates me."

"On the contrary," Hazel said. "She told me she admires your gumption."

"She did?"

"Yes. So don't go jumping to any conclusions. Just wait for Sam to get in touch with you. I'm sure he will."

Laura wished *she* could be sure he would. She was starting to run a little low on gumption.

That night she raided her freezer twice.

The next day was a repeat of the one before, except that Laura limited herself to two calls to Sam's office. Mabel, recognizing Laura's voice immediately, had just said, "He's not here." The second time, however, Mabel's tough voice had actually softened a bit as she'd added, "Be patient."

That sounded as if there might be hope, and Laura felt she could sure use a little hope right about now. Things were starting to look pretty grim, and a little voice in her head whispered that maybe she should leave Baileys Crossing after all.

"Dr. Peters, there's someone here to see you," Hazel called out at the end of the extremely long day.

Laura grimaced. It was the tone of voice Hazel reserved to announce pushy dental supply salesmen. Well, there was no sense putting it off. She'd simply tell the man she wasn't interested in what he was offering.

But when Laura walked into the reception area, she found she was very interested in what *this* man was offering. It was Sam.

"We need to talk," he stated gruffly.

"Okay." Now that he was standing in front of her, wearing his customary jeans and work shirt, all the brilliant words she'd prepared evaporated like water in a desert.

Sam didn't even give Laura time to remove her lab coat as he hustled her downstairs and into his car, which was illegally parked at the curbside. Minutes later they were at the Mitchell and Sons warehouse.

Moving quickly, Sam again hustled her inside to what she assumed to be his office. The place was deserted.

She looked around in confusion. "What are we doing here?"

"This." He pulled her into his arms and kissed her with hungry desperation. It was a complicated kiss, filled with anger and joy, frustration and satisfaction.

Laura held him tightly, almost afraid this was all a dream. She felt his lips soften as he tasted her response. His next kiss was gentler but no less hungry.

"Look," he finally muttered, "I may not be very fancy, and the blinds in this place may be crooked all the time, but I love you."

Laura couldn't follow what he'd said about the blinds, but she didn't care. There were three words he'd said that she'd understood very clearly. He loved her. "Oh, Sam," she murmured unsteadily. "I love you, too!"

Further elaboration wasn't necessary as his mouth covered hers with vibrant passion.

When Laura next came up for air, she realized they were now both sitting—he in an office chair, and she on his lap. Silently, heatedly, he began practicing the gentle art of seduction as she sat there, draped across his thighs. His hands blazed a provocative trail from her shoulder to her hip.

"What do you have in your pocket?" he muttered as his fingers encountered sharp edges in a woman who had none.

"Plastic dinosaurs. For my patients. I keep a few surprises—" she gasped as his hands slid beneath her lab coat to caress the curve of her breast through the thin cotton of her dress "—in my pockets."

"Got any surprises for me?"

"Mmm, plenty." She moved against him, letting him feel how much she wanted him, how much she loved him.

Sam was moving, too, holding her tighter as they shared another fiery kiss. The intensity of their passion made the suddenness of the interruption all the more startling.

"Time's up!" Mabel shouted from outside the door. Coming inside, she eyed the two of them with indulgent disapproval. "I said—time's up."

"Come back tomorrow," Sam growled, refusing to let a flustered Laura get up from his lap.

"Forget it. You two have had enough time to fool around in here. There are things to be done, remember?"

"And I was about to do them when we were so rudely interrupted," Sam retorted.

"Those weren't the kind of things I was talking about and you know it, Samuel Augustus Mitchell!"

"Samuel Augustus, huh?" Laura repeated with interest, her eyes now twinkling in amusement. "You must be Mabel. I'm so glad to meet you."

"Likewise," the older woman said.

"I'd get up but…" Laura indicated Sam's possessive hold on her.

"I understand. That boy always was too charming for his own good."

"See? I'm not the only one who thinks you're charming," Laura loftily informed Sam.

Sam ignored her comment. "We need a few more minutes. There are still some things Laura and I need to discuss."

"Just make sure that's all you do—discuss. 'Cause if you're not outside in ten minutes, I'm sending your mother in," Mabel declared before leaving.

Panicking, Laura practically leaped from Sam's lap. "Your mother?"

"Mabel was just kidding," Sam hastily assured her.

"Why does she want you to go outside?" Laura frowned. "I thought the warehouse was closed."

"The warehouse is closed. I'll explain in a minute. But first I think we should talk."

Laura nodded her agreement. "As Hazel would say, I blew it. I'm sorry. I should have told you everything in the beginning. I did plan on telling you eventually—when it was all over with. I kept hoping there would be some way of fixing it, of making it all right. You might as well know that I really screwed up. I should have anticipated something like this happening, should have made contingency plans. But I didn't. Now I'm paying for my mistake, literally paying for it."

"What makes it your mistake and not your cousin's?" Sam demanded.

"I'm supposed to look out for her."

"And I'd say cosigning a loan for her is looking out for her."

"Not when I didn't do any follow-up work on it. What can I say? I grew up with an overdeveloped sense of responsibility, I guess. As Hazel only recently pointed out to me, I tend to be the first to take the blame when something goes wrong."

"What's this?" Sam said with teasing horror. "Not *more* character flaws?"

She loved him more at that moment than she ever had before. How was it that he always knew what to say to make her feel better? She smiled somewhat unsteadily while admitting, "I guess I'm just not used to making mistakes."

"Well, you'd better get used to making them," Sam replied. "You're only human, you know. I don't expect you to be perfect. I don't *want* you to be perfect. God knows, I'm not. Think how frustrating it would be to live with someone who was always doing everything right." His teasing expression turned serious as he added, "And you can forget trying to go it alone. You've got me in your life now. And that means every part of your life, Laura. I won't settle for anything less," he stated bluntly.

"I realize that now. But still, it's not really fair for you to have to worry about my problems." That aspect of the situation still concerned her.

"Your problems are my problems. Don't you know that by now?"

"Oh, Sam . . ." She blinked away the tears.

He looked at her in dismay. "Hey, you're not gonna cry or anything, are you?"

He sounded so horrified at the prospect that she couldn't help laughing.

"That's better," he said approvingly. "You've got to learn how to accept help without crying."

"I'll work on it," she promised. "It's just that I was raised not to depend on the charity of others."

"You don't have to depend on others. Just me. Because you and I are a team." He brushed his thumb over her parted lips. "That means we face the good and the bad together. Got that?"

She nodded.

"Good," he said briskly. "Then we'd better go. Mabel was right. We're late."

Laura blinked at his sudden change of tone. "Late for what?"

"You'll see. But you won't be needing this anymore today." He efficiently removed the lab coat she'd forgotten about. "Okay, let's go."

Taking her by the hand, Sam led her through the maze-like warehouse to an outdoor area in back. Even from a distance she could see that it was filled with people.

She pulled him to a stop. "I don't understand. I thought you said the warehouse was closed."

"It is closed." He tugged her forward the last few feet so that she could see the hand-painted Save The Smiles banner strung between two piles of lumber. "These people are all here for you. To show their support for you. And to help you the way you've helped them so many times in the past."

Laura looked at all the people gathering around her, barely hearing their applause and cheers. She couldn't believe this was happening. "But how...?" she murmured dazedly.

"How doesn't matter," Sam replied. "The why does. They all wanted to help."

Laura began picking faces out of the crowd. There was Susan Weisman, who hugged her and whispered, "The diorce settlement came through! Finally! Thanks for being o patient about my payment.''

The entire Cho family was there, pleased as punch about Mr. Cho's new job—at none other than Mitchell and Sons.

In fact, she couldn't get over how many of her patients nd their parents were there. Doubting Thomas and his mom, the accident-prone Daryl and his mom. Even Daette the Yodeler with both her parents.

There was only one person who could have notified her atients. Hazel. Sure enough, she was there along with Jerry nd his wife. So was Sandy. They must have left the office ight after she had.

But there were also people who weren't patients. Lilly was here. As was Smitty. And wasn't that Ralph with the infaous bunions over there talking with him? Next to them vas a group of people she knew from the Friends of the Lirary and historical society meetings. There were even peole from the nearby hospital where she gave her prenatal resentations.

Laura was so overwhelmed that tears came to her eyes. he couldn't believe so many people had shown up—for her.

"Okay, gang, let's get the show under way," Mabel delared in a booming voice. The noisy crowd immediately uieted down. "Hazel, if you'd be so kind..."

Nodding, Hazel stepped up into a gazebo that had been et up as a podium. "I promise I'll keep it brief, folks. aura, since you came to Baileys Crossing three years ago, ou've touched us all in a lot of ways. For all those times ou adjusted your fees according to ability to pay, for all the ours of volunteer work you put in, for all the good you've one—we've finally come up with a way to repay you. Inividually we might not have been able to do much, but orking together we were able to raise nine thousand, nine undred and eighty-five dollars!''

Everyone cheered.

"Come on up here, Laura. For all you do, this check's for you!"

Laura was too stunned to move. "It's too much...I can't accept..." she said in a strangled voice.

Sam cut her off by firmly declaring, "Yes, you can. It's not charity, Laura. It's love." He gave her a gentle nudge forward, and the next thing Laura knew she was standing next to a beaming Hazel on the raised floor of the gazebo.

Looking out at the crowd, Laura felt the butterflies attacking her stomach. Her throat closed up, and she couldn't speak. Her frantic eyes fastened on Sam, who stood only a few feet away. Mouthing the words *I love you*, he gave her an intimate smile and a thumbs-up sign.

Suddenly she knew what to say. "I want to thank you all." Her voice was shaky at first, but it soon picked up confidence. "You'll never know how much this means to me." She turned to hug Hazel. Facing forward again, she looked directly at Sam. "And in particular I want to thank one of the smartest men I know—Sam Mitchell. He's taught me many things, but most importantly he's shown me that it's okay to be human. That he'll love me...character flaws—" she used the words deliberately "—and all. That's a wonderful gift to give to somebody." Laura bit her lip as she fought off the tears. "I once told him that I'm not good at expressing my feelings, and I'm not. But I want all of you...and him...to know that I love him more than I have words to say." She held her hand out to him.

Joining her, Sam gave her a hug. "And you said you were no good at giving speeches," he gruffly whispered in her ear. Keeping one arm around her waist, he turned to face the crowd. "Since you've declared your feelings in front of the entire town, it's only fair that I do the same. I love you, Laura Peters. Will you marry me?"

There wasn't a dry eye in the house as Laura confidently made her reply, loud enough that even the people in the back could hear. "Yes!"

Bedlam broke out after that as everyone rushed forward to congratulate the happy couple. Among the first was Sam's family. The introductions were extremely informal as Sam called out their names.

"Younger brother—Joey."

"Way to go, bro!" Joey said, patting Sam so hard on the back he almost knocked him off his feet. Then he shook Laura's hand vigorously. "Nice to meet you, doc."

"His wife, Sally, and their daughter, Kim."

"Welcome to the family," Sally said. The teething Kim grinned and drooled.

"Older brother, Frank, and his wife, Anne."

"Please excuse my rambunctious baby brother, but we've really been looking forward to meeting you," Frank said.

"Yeah," Joey seconded. "We wanted to see the woman who'd knocked our brother off his feet."

"We knew it had to be someone special. Sam's not easily impressed," Anne said.

"What about me, Uncle Sam?" a little voice demanded. Sam scooped his niece Cindy up in his arms. "And you already know this little squirt."

"Yes, indeed." They were the first words Laura had been allowed to get in. "Thank you, Cindy, for bringing your uncle to my office with you."

Cindy smiled shyly and tugged on Sam's shirt collar, her signal that she had something important to whisper in his ear. "I'm glad you're not scared of Dr. Peters anymore. I didn't tell."

"I know you didn't." He gave her a big bear hug. "Thanks, small fry."

"You're welcome, Uncle Sam. And thanks for my kit ten. I love her even better than my baby brother some times."

"So long as it's only sometimes, I guess that's okay," Sam whispered back.

"Put that little girl down and come hug your mother!" Mr. Mitchell bellowed across the distance that separated him from his middle son.

"Hey, Pop, don't you know it's impolite to yell in fron of ladies?"

The others stepped aside so that Sam's parents coul come forward. Laura held her breath as Mr. Mitchell sizee her up. Then he smiled and nodded his head approvingly "So you're the young lady who's stolen my son's heart. It's about time. Congratulations."

The next thing she knew, Laura was enveloped in a bea hug like the one Sam had just given little Cindy.

"Now, Sean," Mrs. Mitchell gently admonished he husband, "don't smother the girl."

When Laura was released from Mr. Mitchell's bone crushing hug, she got her first look at Sam's mother. Sh was a petite woman with a smile that was quietly welcom ing. She didn't look at all like the type of woman to com after anyone with a shotgun. Still, Laura couldn't help th nervous reaction of slipping one hand in her pocket.

Mrs. Mitchell's smile widened. "I think I'm going to lik you," Sam's mother said as she pulled her own hands ou of her pockets and held them both out to Laura. "Takes on to know one, dear," she murmured with a humorousl pointed look at Laura's pocket. "Don't worry. I thin you're going to settle in just fine."

"I hope so. I'll try my best."

"That's good enough for me."

Smiling with relief, Laura put both arms around Sam' mother and hugged her. "Thanks."

"Thank you, dear. I never thought I'd see the day when his one—" Sam's mother cast an affectionately exasperated look at her son "—would settle down. You've no idea the number of gray hairs he's given me."

"I hate to interrupt," Hazel said, "but do you think you could stand to hear some more good news?"

Laura nodded.

"April called right as we were leaving the office. She asked me to give you a message." Efficient as always, Hazel checked the pink phone message slip and read it verbatim. "Good news. The lease is no longer a problem. She'll call you tonight."

"That's great! Thanks, Hazel. And thanks for arranging all this."

"Well, I only helped some. The idea was Sam's. He's the one to thank."

"Oh, I intend to thank him," Laura replied with a heated smile in Sam's direction. "A lot."

He was by her side a moment later. "Think they'll notice we leave?" he whispered in her ear.

"What do you think?"

"That I'm going to go crazy if I don't kiss you soon," Sam muttered.

"What's stopping you?"

"The fact that once I start kissing you, I won't be able to stop."

"I see," she murmured understandingly. "In that case, perhaps it would be wise to wait until we leave."

"And after that?"

"I'll leave it to your imagination," she replied seductively.

Sam's imagination was particularly inspired that evening as he made love to her with glorious passion and pure tenderness. He claimed her as his, loving her not only with his body but with his heart and soul, as well.

Laura responded by gentling him with a kiss, arousin
him with a caress. She gave him provocation and gratifica
tion, promising him heaven and giving it to him. It wasn't
trip he took alone. They both touched the stars that night

Afterward they stayed close, snuggling together in he
double bed.

Threading his fingers through her silken hair, Sam whi
pered, "I never did get around to giving you that blu
nightgown from Lilly's, did I?"

"No, you didn't." She didn't sound very upset about it

Cupping his hand under her chin, he turned her face u
to his. "Don't you want it?"

Laura smiled. "I've got all I ever wanted. I've got you.

*   *   *   *   *

SILHOUETTE® Desire™

COMING NEXT MONTH

577 CANDLELIGHT FOR TWO—Annette Broadrick
Steve Donovan was the last person Jessica Sheldon wanted to accompany her to Australia. Can two people who've made fighting into an art find forever in each other's arms?

578 NOT EASY—Lass Small
Detective Winslow Homer thought finding Penelope Rutherford's missing camera would be a snap. But it wasn't so easy—and neither was getting Penelope to admit that she found him irresistible!

579 ECHOES FROM THE HEART—Kelly Jamison
Brenna McShane had never forgotten her very sexy—and very unreliable—ex-husband. Then Luke McShane returned, bringing some all the remembered pain . . . and all the remembered passion of their young love.

580 YANKEE LOVER—Beverly Barton
Historian Laurel Drew was writing her ancestor's biography when unrefined John Mason showed up with a different story. Soon sparks were flying between this Southern belle and her Yankee lover.

581 BETWEEN FRIENDS—Candace Spencer
When reasonable Logan Fletcher proposed marriage to his best friend, Catherine Parrish, it wasn't for love. Could he ever understand Catherine's utterly romantic reasons for accepting?

582 HOTSHOT—Kathleen Korbel
July's *Man of the Month*, photojournalist Devon Kane liked to be where the action was. But with his latest subject—reclusive Libby Matthews—Devon found the greatest adventure was love!

AVAILABLE NOW:

You'll flip . . . your pages won't!
Read paperbacks *hands-free* with

Book Mate · I

The perfect "mate" for all your romance paperbacks
Traveling • Vacationing • At Work • In Bed • Studying
• Cooking • Eating

Perfect size for all standard paperbacks, this wonderful invention makes reading a pure pleasure! Ingenious design holds paperback books OPEN and FLAT so even wind can't ruffle pages— leaves your hands free to do other things. Reinforced, wipe-clean vinyl-covered holder flexes to let you turn pages without undoing the strap . . . supports paperbacks so well, they have the strength of hardcovers!

Pages turn WITHOUT opening the strap.

SEE-THROUGH STRAP

Reinforced back stays flat

Built in bookmark

BOOK MARK

BACK COVER HOLDING STRIP

10˝ x 7¼˝, opened.
Snaps closed for easy carrying, too

Silhouette Romance®

CIMARRON STORIES

A TRILOGY BY PEPPER ADAMS

Pepper Adams is back and spicier than ever with three tender, heartwarming tales, set on the plains of Oklahoma.

CIMARRON KNIGHT ... available in June
Rugged rancher and dyed-in-the-wool bachelor Brody Sawyer meets his match in determined Noelle Chandler and her adorable twin boys!

CIMARRON GLORY ... available in August
With a stubborn streak as strong as her foster brother Brody's, Glory Roberts has her heart set on lassoing handsome loner Ross Forbes ... and uncovering his mysterious past....

CIMARRON REBEL ... available in October
Brody's brother Riley is a handsome rebel with a cause! And he doesn't mind getting roped into marrying Darcy Durant—in name only—to gain custody of two heartbroken kids.

**Don't miss CIMARRON KNIGHT, CIMARRON GLORY and
CIMARRON REBEL—three special stories that'll win your
heart ... available only from Silhouette Romance!**